C'EST LA VIE

FACT, FICTION, AND FANTASY

MARIE CUNNINGHAM DAVIDSON

BALBOA
PRESS

A DIVISION OF HAY HOUSE

Balboa Press books may be ordered through booksellers or by contacting:

Balboa Press
A Division of Hay House
1663 Liberty Drive
Bloomington, IN 47403
www.balboapress.com.au
1 (877) 407-4847

Print information available on the last page.

ISBN: 978-1-5043-1324-7 (sc)
ISBN: 978-1-5043-1325-4 (e)

Balboa Press rev. date: 05/30/2018

I dedicate this book to my amazing mother,
Marjorie Cunningham, for her strength and
determination against all odds.
9 November 1935 – 25 May 2018

Be mindful when it comes to your words. A string of some that don't mean much to you, may stick with someone else for a lifetime.

—Rachel Wolchin

CONTENTS

OUTBACK TERROR

INTRODUCTION

Melbourne is the capital city of Victoria, Australia. Australia is a large island continent, mainly inhabited along the coastlines. However, in Victoria and New South Wales, there are many regional centres and tiny townships which make up these states. There are also many long and lonely roads connecting the towns. My journey was about six hundred kilometres, from Melbourne to Mildura, one of Victoria's largest regional centres. From there, I would drive another six hundred kilometres to Whyalla, in South Australia. The journey was mostly on quiet highways with not much traffic. I had made the trip many times previously but had never had a scary trip like this one before! This is based on a true story.

CHAPTER 1

THE JOURNEY BEGINS

It was six o'clock in the morning when I left Melbourne. Half awake, even after three cups of strong coffee, I set off from home. I had arranged to spend the weekend with my sister Susan in Mildura. It was great getting together. Unfortunately, this was something we were unable to do often. When we did, we usually had a few glasses of red wine, perhaps a nice Merlot from an Australian winery named the Four Sisters (we are a four-sister family, so it was special), and a sing-song on the back veranda of her homestead in Merbein, just outside of Mildura.

Susan was the coordinator of a childcare facility, and her partner, George, was a primary school teacher. I was also looking forward to spending time with their two gorgeous kids, Toby and Jean. From Merbein, I was heading over to Whyalla, in South Australia, to catch up with the rest of the family.

I have no idea why I headed for Ballarat that day. It was probably a result of my being tired. Normally, I would travel this way to drive to Adelaide. So it may have been from habit. On the road, I was singing to wake myself up. Suddenly, I realised I was heading in the wrong direction. Instead of going west, I should have been travelling north. Quickly, I pulled over to the side of the road and turned on my GPS.

Sure enough, I was heading for Ballarat, whereas I should have been heading for Bendigo. I'd now have to travel cross-country on very small, barely used roads.

I reached Newbury before travelling cross-country to get back to the original route and on to Highway 79, headed north to Mildura. This mistake had added two hours to my overall journey. Still feeling very tired, I pulled in to a roadhouse in the small town of Winchester for some brunch.

The sign informed me that Winchester had a population of 130. After ordering a sandwich and a drink, I asked the guy behind the counter if there were any parks in the town where I could go to eat my lunch. He said that there were plenty of parks in the town and that they were easy to find if I just drove around. Actually, he was a bit creepy. It wasn't anything in particular that he'd said. He just creeped me out.

Settling back into my car, I drove around the town, which was deserted. It was forty degrees already, and the day was getting warmer by the minute. I guessed everyone was inside with the air conditioning turned up. There were numerous parks, but the picnic tables were right in the middle of them. The parks were really quiet and isolated, so I decided to eat my food in the car and then head off.

I had been driving for about fifteen minutes when I noticed a car in my rear-vision mirror. At first, the car followed at a distance, and then it commenced driving right up to the rear of my vehicle, before pulling off again. The car was green, but I couldn't see much of the driver—just that he was wearing very dark aviator sunglasses.

I didn't take too much notice initially, but after he'd tailgated me and then backed off five or six times, I got a bit nervous. I was on a quiet country road, with no one within "cooee", so I felt isolated.

I decided I had to get rid of this pesky driver. Pulling into another roadhouse in the next small town, I ordered a coffee and a slice of cake and sat for a while. I allowed the nuisance driver to overtake me so I could resume my journey without the hassle of him following me.

CHAPTER 2

WEDDERBURN

While I had stopped at the roadhouse, allowing my nuisance driver to pass me, I tried to read his registration plates, but that was difficult because I didn't want him to see my face. All I managed were the first two letters: RW. I did take note, however, that the car was green and was a Toyota, perhaps a hatchback.

A cup of strong coffee was in order—not this time to keep me awake, but to calm my nerves. This idiot had me a little rattled, I had to admit. After ordering coffee and a buttered finger bun, I sat and thought about what was happening here.

Not much really. Then why was I so spooked? This mystery driver had followed me for about fifty kilometres, tailgating me and then dropping back, over and over again. I tried to rationalise it. Probably some bored teenager was playing chicken with me for as long as he could get away with it. Had I been in the city, I would have jumped out and given him a piece of my mind. But I wasn't in the city. I was in the middle of nowhere, and he knew it. Maybe he was trying to run me off the road, and then maybe he'd—

Stop it, I told myself. I just knew I was getting myself all worked up over nothing.

I tried to convince myself that this was all in my imagination. Why would he choose me to play silly road games with? There was no reason for me to get panicky over this. I needed to get back into my car and just get on with the rest of the journey.

After finishing my coffee and my finger bun, which was really tasty and gave me a sugar boost, I found that I was no longer tired. By then I was alert and anxious to reach Susan's place in Mildura as quickly as I could. Dropping my waste in a rubbish bin, I hopped into the car and resumed my journey.

He'll be well gone by now, I thought. *Keep up a steady speed and you won't catch up with him. You'll be fine!*

Observing the speed limit, I exited the town and started out onto the main highway. I felt good because there were no other cars in either direction. I started to sing "Ben" along with Michael Jackson. *That's an oldie but a goodie,* I thought.

As I thought this, I glanced into my rear-view mirror and—

No, this is not possible. I watched him drive past me at the roadhouse. How can he be behind me again? I sped up, and he dropped back.

Okay, I'll drive as fast as the speed limit will allow me. That will get me ahead of him.

Looking in the rear-view mirror and realising he was tailgating me again, I thought I was going mad.

Why is he following me? What purpose does it serve? None. He is either just playing with me, or he means me harm!

Stop it! You're just frightening yourself for no reason.

So I flattened my foot and accelerated to 130 kilometres an hour, thinking he'd never catch up with me at that rate. I was driving a Mazda 3 SP25, which I knew could handle two hundred kilometres per hour. I didn't intend to drive at that speed, but I took some comfort in the knowledge that I could probably outrun him if I needed to.

Flabbergasted, I checked the rear-view mirror and there he

was—about eight metres behind me. I tried to note anything of the driver or the car that I could. There was a yellow strip hanging from his rear-view mirror. He had a dark, swarthy complexion, perhaps Mediterranean or Middle Eastern, with dark aviator sunglasses. He was so close that I could see that he wasn't clean-shaven.

Am I just imagining this? Maybe I'm going mad.

I was approaching Wedderburn, still six hours out of Mildura. I had to get rid of this idiot once and for all. So stopping at the town, I once again allowed the green car to pass me, catching another letter of his registration plate as he passed by: RWD.

Taking my time, I topped up the fuel tank, checked the water levels of my car, checked the tyres, and added some air to one tyre, which had deflated a little. It wasn't a real issue, but it gave me time to let this idiot driver get well ahead of me.

After entering the roadhouse, I paid for my fuel and ordered a sandwich and a cup of tea. I took my time, waiting until I thought the road was clear. I allowed half an hour to pass before taking off towards Mildura.

CHAPTER 3

ON THE ROAD AGAIN

Following the sixty-kilometre-per-hour limit out of Wedderburn, I gradually increased my speed until I was on Highway 79 once again. I dreaded looking in my rear-vision mirror, but the road behind me seemed clear.

Phew! Thank goodness for that, I thought. *I don't think I could have taken much more.*

About twenty kilometres out of Wedderburn, I glanced behind again. *I don't believe this! I thought I gave him a half-hour head start on me. What's going on?*

This time, there was no doubting it. I had left this guy at Wedderburn and allowed him half an hour's grace before heading off again. He couldn't be behind me. It must be someone else. But checking my rear-vision mirror confirmed that this was the same driver, in the same car that had been following me for the past eighty kilometres.

Perhaps it's a mistake, I thought. *I must be imagining this. I'm going crazy.*

No, I wasn't mistaken, and I wasn't crazy. The driver zoomed up, almost touching my rear bumper bar. Then he dropped back ten metres or so and did it all over again. This continued for another twenty kilometres or so. I was getting scared.

What is he going to do next?

But he didn't change his pattern at all, accelerating up until almost touching my car, and then dropping back. I tried speeding up, but he matched my speed. Then I tried slowing down, but he wouldn't overtake me.

How had he managed to get behind me anyway? He must have hidden around the corner and watched me leave Wedderburn. Then he must have waited until I'd left the speed zone for the town, before following me again.

Why? I pondered. My thoughts turned to the backpacker murders and the Truro murders—true stories about young people being taken on lonely country roads. *Oh my God, what if he's a murderer?* Then I thought I needed to take it easy. Apart from tailgating me, he hadn't done anything to threaten me, had he?

Just as I had this thought, the green hatchback that had followed me for nearly a hundred and thirty kilometres suddenly overtook me. *What now?*

Without warning, he slammed on his brakes and pulled over to the side of the road. Through the dust, I saw him fling open his driver's-side door. I reacted instinctively, swerving around his door, but I was shaking; I could feel the terror creeping in.

Jeez, that was scary!

I peeked in my rear-view mirror and saw that he didn't get out of the car but just sat there staring at me as I headed off into the distance. I thought this was good, that his car had probably broken down: wishful thinking!

Trying to keep both eyes on the road, I turned the next bend, and when I looked up again I flashed to my rear-vision mirror. *Oh my God, what's happening?* There he was, not ten metres behind me.

So the "game" took on another strategy. He would tailgate me and then drop back ten or twenty metres, and then suddenly he'd be almost touching my rear bumper bar again. Every now and then, he would accelerate, overtake me, and slam on the brakes, flinging open his door. I would once again swerve to miss his car and accelerate, leaving him behind, until he caught up with me again. I was lucky that there was no traffic coming in the other direction; the result would have been catastrophic.

I was really scared by now, but I didn't know what to do. Ring the police? I'd feel like an idiot. My story was so crazy that they would probably think I was mad.

The town of Boigbeat was about twenty minutes away.

I've made it this far, I thought. *I can make it to the next town.*

Deciding to have another long break, I hoped again that he would lose interest in me. In the meantime he kept up his routine of tailgate, drop back, tailgate, then overtake and make me swerve to avoid him.

I have to admit I was really scared by this time. He'd been following me for over 150 kilometres. The stress was showing, through stiffness in my neck and arms, and a splitting headache that wouldn't abate.

My heart lifted as I saw the sign "Boigbeat, five kilometres". Trying to ignore the idiot on my tail, I focussed instead on a hot cup of tea and a break from the stress of this nightmare.

Drawing in to Boigbeat, I quickly located a roadhouse and climbed out of my car, keeping my eyes down and surreptitiously taking note of his registration number as he flew past me. "RWD" was all I managed to see.

The day was dragging on. At this rate it would be late afternoon before I reached Mildura, but I needed to try to put some distance between me and the green hatchback, so I ordered a cup of tea and a biscuit and sat down to wait for half an hour before hitting the road again.

I used the restroom, pausing to wash my face with cold water. I dried off with paper towels and felt a little refreshed.

While at the roadhouse, I checked the large map of Victoria on the wall. I verified that I had been followed for over 150 kilometres, and I was convinced that this guy who was following me was a mate of the creepy guy at the roadhouse in Winchester.

I knew he was sleazy and creepy; I just didn't know what gave me that feeling. I could just imagine him getting on the phone to his creepy mate and telling him I was alone and driving on Route 79 to Mildura. This horror story only started after I'd left Winchester.

I was angry at the driver of the green car for making me feel afraid on the road, for tailgating me, and for putting my life at risk by forcing me to swerve to avoid his open car door. The more I thought about it, the angrier I became—and the more determined that I wouldn't let him beat me. What I didn't know was that when I left Boigbeat, things were about to get a whole lot worse.

Sitting in the roadhouse at Boigbeat, I watched the second hand on the clock move as if in slow motion. I needed to wait half an hour, and I was anxious to reach Mildura in one piece. That was the problem: I didn't know for sure that I'd reach Mildura, let alone intact. Seriously worried by this time, I thought about phoning the police, but I feared being labelled a crackpot. After all, he hadn't exactly harmed me. No, I wouldn't do it just yet. I kept thinking I was imagining it all.

I still had two hundred kilometres to cover that day, and all of these stops were dragging the day out. I knew that it would be late afternoon, at that rate, before I arrived. Thank goodness for daylight saving, as it would still be light until nine thirty in the evening.

I finished my tea and watched the news on the screen in the roadhouse. Everything was doom and gloom, so I switched it off. I kept imagining myself being a body found on the side of Highway 79 to Mildura. I shuddered.

I waited exactly thirty minutes, and then I used the conveniences, once again washing my face with cold water. It was a hot day outside and my lips tasted salty. Looking in the mirror, I realised that I looked exhausted and had puffy bags under my eyes. I needed to get to Mildura as quickly as possible.

On the road again, I once again waited until I was outside the city limits to put my foot to the floor and zoom myself out onto the highway and resume my journey to Mildura.

The next stretch was a difficult one. The roads were winding, and there were often kangaroos and sheep on the highway looking for water. It was ninety kilometres to the next main town of Ouyen, about an hour away if I were left in peace by Mr Green, car stalker.

I couldn't believe it: at the very moment that thought entered my head, I glanced up at my rear-view mirror and saw the grille of his bonnet grinning up at me.

What the …? How did he get behind me again, and why? What sort of sicko gets his kicks from following women in cars on outback roads?

The movie *Jindabyne* flashed into my head. I started to shake.

This was ridiculous. It had to be my imagination … But then something caught my eye up ahead. There was a blue Holden station wagon in front of me, travelling at about 80 kilometres an hour instead of the posted limit of 110.

Glancing in the rear-view mirror, I could see Mister Green creeping up behind me. The blue Holden wasn't going any faster, so I became wedged between the two. The road was very winding and I was trapped. I tried to get Mister Blue to increase his speed by flashing my lights, but to no avail.

Then it occurred to me: these two were working together.

I thought, *Oh my God, what am I going to do?*

We drove like that for another twenty kilometres, until Mister Blue was driving at about forty kilometres per hour. I thought, *Fuck this for a joke. I'm getting out of here.*

So I overtook Mister Blue and left him for dead, zooming off down the highway with no respect for any speed limit. I had to put some real distance between me and these two jokers. I was almost hoping I would be pulled over by the highway patrol, so they could catch these idiots red-handed.

All went quiet for about ten minutes. I slowed back down to the speed limit. Billy Joel's "Piano Man" came on the radio, so I joined in, knowing that music soothes the soul. I was really getting into it when I glanced up at the rear-vision mirror.

I couldn't believe this.

"Why are you frigging doing this to me!" I screamed at the driver of the green car behind me, who obviously couldn't hear me at all. I was dreadfully tired and emotionally drained.

I couldn't handle much more of this, so I started to cry, sobbing uncontrollably. But the crying was slowing me down and I had to get away from this pair. Nothing good would come of me losing control at that stage. I took a deep breath and pulled myself together as best I could.

It was only about twenty kilometres from Ouyen. I decided to stick it out and then have a rest break there and see if I could work out where they had hidden each time I had stopped. Mr Green continued to play games with me by driving up, almost touching my car, and then dropping back ten or twenty feet before accelerating again. Then occasionally he would overtake me and slam on the brakes on the side of the road, creating a dust storm, preventing me from gaining any visual clues as to his identity. When he threw open the driver's-side door, I swerved, trying to avoid hitting his car door. And in the process at one point, I nearly wiped out another car.

This was no longer a joke, nor a figment of my imagination. I was being dangerously stalked. This could all end very badly for me.

Mister Blue was nowhere in sight, so I conceded that maybe he wasn't involved in this nightmare after all. I rounded a bend. Then, glancing in the rear-vision mirror, I could see Mister Blue, behind Mister Green.

They took it in turns and changed places so that one or the other could creep up behind me, then fall back about twenty feet. Mister Green overtook me, slammed on the brakes in the dirt on the side of the road, and flung his door open. I realised that there was a car coming in the opposite direction. I needed to slow down to avoid a collision.

It seemed to happen in slow motion. I looked across at Mister Green and he stared at me with a face devoid of expression. With dark aviator sunglasses and a five o'clock shadow, he looked as I'd originally thought, Middle Eastern or maybe Mediterranean.

Then I was speeding up and away from them both. Glancing back, I saw Mister Blue had slowed down to allow Mister Green to resume his place behind me.

Maybe he is involved!

I was so sick of this. I didn't care anymore; I just wanted them gone.

The town of Ouyen was a welcome sight. I pulled into the roadhouse there and drove straight to the petrol bowser so I could see the road and try to determine the last registration number as Mister Green passed me. I also wanted to try to see where he was heading, where he would be lying in wait for me.

Sure enough he didn't drive on out of town but instead turned into a side street about five hundred metres away. He must have done a U-turn and parked so that just the nose of the car peeked out from the corner. I'd recognise that car anywhere! The digit on the registration plate that I'd been missing was a 5; at least now I had the complete registration.

I wasn't hungry and had just ordered a strong coffee. While I was drinking it, I contemplated my next move. I needed to phone Susan; she would know what to do.

Heading back to my car, I covertly scanned the street and noticed that Mr Green was still parked at the corner. *I'd love to turn this whole thing back on you, jerk*, I thought.

Screw you!

Turning the car on, I used my hands-free phone system to call Susan's number. I was very disappointed when I reached her message bank.

"You have reached the message bank for Susan and George. We'd love to talk to you, so please leave your name, your phone number, and a short message, and we'll contact you as soon as possible."

Susan was probably at karate, I thought, as they usually trained on Saturdays. After leaving a message, I tried to decide whether to continue or to wait until I'd spoken to her.

I left a message: "Hi, Susie, it's Julie. I'm on my way, as you know, but there's a bit of a weirdo who's been following me and I don't know what to do. Can you please call me back? Love you, Sis."

I could have called 0-0-0, but what was my emergency? Mister Green had been following me but hadn't actually hurt me in any way. He had just frightened me. And the addition of Mister Blue to the equation had just heightened my distress. I felt I would sound like a neurotic female just seeking attention.

Feeling better that I'd actually told someone, I thought that Susan wouldn't judge me and would probably convince me to call the police.

I was faced with a dilemma about what to do: take off again, or wait for Susie's call?

CHAPTER 4

HELP IS ON ITS WAY

Sitting in my car and listening to the radio while waiting for Susan to call me back, I was able to keep an eye on Mister Green's car. He hadn't moved, but I couldn't see whether Mister Blue was behind him.

Okay, just stay where you are, I thought. *You'll get what's coming to you, you creep.*

I was getting a bit cocky, though I wasn't contemplating going any further without help from someone, whether Susan or the police, or both.

After half an hour, though, I started to get restless and thought about making a mad dash for Mildura at top speed, leaving these clowns in my dust.

Yeah, and you're dreaming, woman! I told myself.

Just then the phone rang. I turned my engine over and my call went to hands-free.

"Susie?"

"Julie, what's going on?"

I laughed sheepishly. "It's probably just my imagination, but I think I have a stalker following me," I told her.

"Where? How long for? Where are you?" I should have known she would panic.

"Susie, it's probably nothing, but I think that a car has been following me since Winchester, and I'm now at Ouyen!" I explained.

"Winchester? What were you doing in Winchester?"

"It's a long story. I took a wrong turn. Then this creepy guy appeared who's been stalking me ever since," I told her.

"So you've rung the police?"

"Well, no."

"Why not? Are you crazy? Haven't you seen *Wolf Creek?*"[1]

"What's *Wolf Creek?*"

"It's a movie about …"

"No, don't tell me. I hate those movies."

"Julie, this is really serious. Why haven't you called the police?"

"Because I feel like a neurotic female who's been spooked by a couple of kids."

"A couple of kids? I thought you said a car was following you?"

"There was one car. Now there's two. And they have been taking it in turns to spook me."

---

[1] A synopsis of *Wolf Creek:* Three friends embark on an adventure in the rugged Australian outback, having set out to see the famous Wolf Creek—a crater made by a meteor thousands of years ago. They spend time partying and bonding during their road trip to the landmark. When they arrive, they leave their car at the bottom to make the three-hour hike to the top of the crater. Upon their return to the car, they find that it will not start, and must enlist the help of a seemingly charitable fellow, who happens to "coincidentally" be meandering around one of the most remote areas of the world. They decide to allow him to tow them and their car back to his dwelling, where he has promised to quickly fix the car. However, the three soon realise he has other plans in store, when, after being drugged, they awake to scenes of terror, grisly dismemberment, and even death. We get to know the three on a personal level, so that what happens to them is more than mere gore and torture; we actually feel for these characters and want them to succeed. A surprisingly well-done, yet very difficult, film to watch.

"Oh my God, Julie, this is serious. Hang up. I'm ringing the police."

"Wait, maybe I'm just imagining things," I said. I glanced over at Mr Green's car, still peeping around the corner, and realised that I wasn't imagining things. I was terrified. Suddenly the dam broke and I was sobbing uncontrollably, hiccupping and trying to talk to Susan at the same time.

She calmed me down and asked for details of my car. I told her that I was in my own charcoal-coloured Mazda, and gave her the registration. Susan then asked me if I was safe at present, and I told her that I was in front of a roadhouse in my car and quite safe as long as I didn't go anywhere.

Giving her the details of the green car, I started to feel a little calmer. As far as I could ascertain, it was a green Toyota Seca hatchback, with the number plate RWD215. I described the driver as thirty to forty years of age, stocky, with a swarthy appearance, not that I could see much, because he was wearing large, dark aviator sunglasses. Then I realised that he also had black hair and a black moustache.

There weren't any details about the blue car, except that it was a Holden station wagon of some sort. I had no idea about the registration number.

I really did feel calmer once I had imparted all of this information. I realised that I was going to be okay.

Susan said that she was going to contact Mildura police and get them to find out which town had their local police station manned at that time.

"I want you to stay exactly where you are. What is the name of the roadhouse?"

"Ricky's," I replied.

"Okay, I'll get the police to meet you outside the roadhouse. And I'll drive down to meet you so we can drive back together."

"You don't have to do that. I'll be okay."

"I do have to do it, and you would do it for me," Susan replied. "Now hang up and I'll call the police."

"Okay, Susie, thank you so much. I should have done this hours ago. I just felt like I was making a mountain out of a molehill."

"Stay there, Sis. I'll see you in an hour."

"Bye, Susie. Thanks. Love you."

"Love you too."

I felt deserted as I cut off the phone, but I knew that Susan would be good to her word and that the police would arrive soon. Heaving a sigh of relief, I settled further into my seat and waited for the police.

CHAPTER 5

THE CAVALRY ARRIVES

The police were there within ten minutes. The officers took my details and those of the green car. I went to point him out, parked down the road, and realised that he had gone. *Smart move*, I thought. *Of course he took off as soon as the police arrived.* I apologised to the police, saying that they probably wouldn't find the two men now that they had taken flight. The police were fantastic, calming me down and promising to keep an eye out.

"Don't ever apologise for calling us out," the older one said. "We'd rather get a call out for nothing than have you going missing. Anything can happen on these country roads. And hoons playing games don't usually follow you for such a long distance."

It was about two hundred kilometres from Winchester to Ouyen. I shuddered as I thought of what could actually have happened to me.

The police, eager to get after the two drivers, headed towards Mildura to see if they could catch up with them. The phone rang a few minutes later: Mildura Police Station.

"Are you sure that was the registration number of the car?" the duty sergeant asked me.

"Yes, I'm pretty sure. I've taken it in parts throughout the day, so I'm pretty sure. Why?"

Marie Cunningham Davidson

"There's no such registration number, so they were false plates. Could it have been a station wagon?"

"No, it was definitely a hatchback," I replied. "Why?"

"There was a registration number that was close, but it was for a green station wagon." He went on to explain to me that there were lots of cars that were unregistered on the farms throughout the area, and that the kids used them to learn to drive, or to drive around the farm and locally. That made sense. So these plates were likely to have been cancelled years before but not surrendered for disposal.

There hadn't been any similar reports, but the officer said that like me, many people were too embarrassed to report incidents like this to the police, so accurate numbers were not known. They would certainly keep my complaint on file, and if any other episodes occurred, they may need to call me for a written statement. I hung up the phone and felt exhausted. In a few minutes, I knew that Susan would be there to drive the rest of the journey in convoy. Heaving a sigh of relief, I locked all of my doors and allowed my eyes to close for a few minutes.

I must have drifted off to sleep, because a few minutes later I was awakened by someone rapping on the window. I practically jumped out of my skin …

CHAPTER 6

SAFE AT LAST

I blinked a couple of times, and the most welcome sight greeted me. "Sis!" I cried. I was out of the car and hugging my sister for all I was worth. "Thank you so much for driving down. Hi, Toby. Hello, Jeannie. Oh, it's so good to see you all."

I didn't want to hang around the roadhouse any longer. I declined the offered cup of coffee, preferring instead to drive to Mildura as soon as possible. Jean drove with me, and Toby stayed with his mum.

I was pretty sure that the police turning up had frightened off my stalkers, but I still felt nervous for the rest of the journey, and found myself constantly checking the rear-vision mirror and worrying about cars coming from the opposite direction. It took just under an hour for us to reach Merbein, right on the outskirts of Mildura. Their property was a couple of acres, so we were quite isolated.

I jumped out of the car, warned Jean to block her ears, and screamed at the top of my lungs.

Oh, that felt good. All of the frustrations of an entire day's travel came hurling out of my mouth. It felt as though I was regurgitating the events of the day.

Susan's car was only five minutes behind mine. After she jumped out, we hugged. I could feel the shaking in my body slowing down, until it disappeared completely.

"Come on inside. I'll put the kettle on and you can tell me the whole story."

I thought about unpacking the car and then gave up on the idea, thinking I'd do it later, after everything calmed down. I grabbed Toby and Jean, hugging them both close to me, and we headed inside.

Susan and George owned a gorgeous hundred-year-old homestead-style house. It was made of weatherboard timber, and had a return veranda. The veranda was about three metres deep, and offered lovely shade around the house on hot days, which were common in Mildura. Summer temperatures soared well into the forties.

We took our tea and a piece of cake out to the veranda to relax and put some distance between us and the kids, so I could talk freely to Susan.

"What on earth happened today?"

I took a deep breath. "I really don't know what started it, Susie, but I've never been so scared in my life." I went on to explain that I'd taken the wrong turn on the freeway and ended up in Winchester; and about the creepy guy in the roadhouse; and how I'd felt while driving around the town.

"I was only a short way out of Winchester when the guy in the green car started following me," I explained. Then I told her about the way he would drive up, almost touching my car, and then drop back. I mentioned how I'd waited in the next town for half an hour but still found him behind me when I resumed my journey.

"Wow, just like *Wolf Creek*." Susan was horrified. "Why didn't you call the police?"

"Susie, I was so worried that I was imagining the whole thing that I was too embarrassed to call the police. What on earth is *Wolf Creek* anyway?"

"It's a movie about a guy who stalks …"

"Wait, don't tell me. I still have to drive to Whyalla in a few days. I'd rather not know."

"You'll be safe. You can just take the back roads," Susie innocently suggested.

"You've got to be kidding. Where do you think this whole thing started?"

Just then the phone rang. Susan ran inside to catch it.

"It's Sergeant Snow, Julie. He wants to talk to you." Susan handed me the phone.

"Hello, Julie speaking."

"Hi, Julie, this is Sergeant Snow from Mildura Police Station. I wanted to catch up with you to make sure that you are okay."

"I'm really shaken," I replied, "but glad to have arrived safely in Mildura. Did you catch them?"

He paused before replying. "No, I'm sorry to say we couldn't find them on the road to Mildura. But they may well have headed back down south, if that's where they started to follow you from."

"It was only one car to begin with, and then the other driver joined in after Wedderburn, I think. Gosh, it's all like a bad dream. I should have rung earlier, but I was too embarrassed."

"Don't ever hesitate to call us if you are travelling alone on country roads. Nine times out of ten it's just some idiot hoon playing chicken with you, but on the odd occasion that it's not … well, we'd rather be safe than sorry."

"I wouldn't hesitate again," I said. "I think I learnt my lesson today."

"Good idea," Sergeant Snow agreed. He took some of my details and said that if anything turned up, he'd give me a call. It was unlikely, he said, speculating that the driver had either changed his registration plates by now or was back on his property with the vehicle hidden away.

The sergeant felt that the second driver was probably a kid who joined his mate for a bit of fun. We had no details about the blue car anyway, so there was nothing to follow up on.

"How long will you be staying in Mildura?"

"I'm in Merbein until Monday, so three days, and then I'm heading off to Whyalla."

"Another long trip. Well, just be careful, and ring if you are worried at all on the road. Do you have a GPS on your car?"

"Yes, why?"

"Because you can give us your exact position if you ever get in a fix." He explained how to access this information from my GPS. You learn something new every day!

Sergeant Snow took the rest of my details, including my home phone number, my address back in Melbourne, and the address where I'd be staying in Whyalla. He was so helpful and concerned that I wished I had called earlier in the day. Here I'd been worried that I'd be embarrassed for ringing the police, and now I felt embarrassed because I hadn't. It was a lesson learnt the hard way.

Susan and I took the kids out for a chocolate milkshake and a walk through the park. Toby and Jean ran on ahead, and Susan and I continued our conversation about what had happened that day.

"You were so lucky, Julie."

"Yes, I think I get that now. Anything could have happened out there. I'd never leave it that long before ringing the police if it happened again."

"In *Wolf Creek* …" she started.

"I don't want to know, Susie. Those films terrify me. And I still have to get to Whyalla."

"Okay, let's grab some food from the supermarket and head home. We can pick up a couple of bottles of Four Sisters at the same time."

Toby and Jean ran ahead again, tagging each other, and then laughed and ran off ahead once more. They were great kids, so easy to entertain.

We finished the day off with a barbecue on the veranda and a couple of glasses of red wine, before seeing the kids off to bed. It was about ten o'clock that night and we were still talking about what had happened that day. George was away fishing. The wine had taken the edge off. We had a laugh about family events from years before. Susan grabbed her guitar and we had a sing-song on the back veranda. It was a glorious night. Revved up by the wine and the events of the day, we were probably a little noisier than usual.

We thought we weren't harming anyone. Then as loud as thunder, a shotgun rang out in the night. Once, twice … Susan and I looked at each other, eyes wide with fright, and ran inside.

Because we were alone on the property, Susan thought it wise to call her nearest neighbour, who lived about two kilometres away. They had heard it too. They decided that it was probably old Louis, who had the block behind Susan, on the other side of the waterway. She hung up the phone and looked at me. We burst out laughing.

"Someone didn't like our singing."

"What a bloody day."

CHAPTER 7

THE JOURNEY CONTINUES

The next few days in Mildura passed quickly. We heard no more of gunshots; however, Louis certainly was working on his property and he was known to shoot at cats and dogs (whether they were wild or not) that ventured on to his property.

We swam in the River Murray with the kids and joined a lunch cruise on the Sunday. It was all perfect, after the crazy start to the long weekend. There was a music festival where we took in a couple of the local bands, which was very pleasant. Susan had stopped talking about *Wolf Creek* and I had stopped talking about the stalkers. I still had five hundred kilometres to drive to Whyalla and I didn't want or need to be spooked further.

After a wonderful weekend, I repacked the car, hugged Susan, Toby, and Jean goodbye, and headed out on the next leg of my journey. I was dreadfully nervous and imagined that people were looking at me as they passed me or as I passed them. If anyone got too close, I felt nervous. I either planted my foot or else slowed down to let them pass me. I needn't have worried; Mister Blue and Mister Green had long since disappeared.

Nonetheless, I took the longer, more travelled route which took me almost to Adelaide. As a result, the roads were busier and I felt less secluded. After a short stop at Port Wakefield for lunch, I completed my journey and was in Whyalla by mid-afternoon. Arriving safely, I dropped in to see my mother in her independent living unit at the Whyalla Foreshore. Mum had a view from her lounge window that Sydneysiders would pay millions for.

I didn't tell Mum about the stalker for many years. I didn't want her to worry any more than she already did. I had a fourteen-hundred-kilometre journey home to Melbourne coming up, and she was worried enough about me making the journey alone. My sisters Connie and Louise, on the other hand, were buzzing with questions about the adventure, their eyes wide with horror when I recounted the events of the day.

"Oh my God," Connie exclaimed, "that's just like *Wolf Creek*, where the …"

"I don't want to know," I replied, fingers in my ears. "I still have to drive back to Melbourne."

"Sorry, but the similarities are astounding."

"I still don't want to know."

"Okay, we won't bring it up again. But promise us that if this ever happens again, you will call the police straightaway," Louise added.

"I absolutely promise."

Both Connie and Louise gave me a big hug. We talked about other things while sipping our Four Sisters.

The next few days passed too quickly, as usual, and soon it was time to leave Whyalla to head back to Melbourne. It was a long trip. I usually broke it up with a night at Gawler, in the Barossa Valley, South Australia, where it was nice to catch up with my brother Joe and his wife Carrie.

We have a "grapevine" in our family, the Channing family. It's called the "Channing-vine," and it is so powerful that it's been known to expose secrets in the United Kingdom before we find out about something that's happened in Adelaide. The Channing-vine was buzzing. I arrived at Gawler to a barrage of questions about my mystery stalkers.

I was really growing tired of this story. Repeating it for the umpteenth time, and answering numerous questions, I then placed a ban on the whole subject. I thought that were I to hear another person mention *Wolf Creek*, I'd scream.

Still, they were my family and they were concerned. I needed to cut them a little slack. We enjoyed a few glasses of red wine and discussed that year's Christmas plans, which included family dinner at Joe and Carrie's place. To be certain, I rang Rod and asked whether he was interested in Christmas in Gawler. After receiving the expected road safety tips from my husband, I settled down for the evening to watch a movie. It was most definitely not *Wolf Creek*.

Early the next day, I set off on my trip back to Melbourne. Deciding to split the trip into two parts, I booked a hotel room at Bordertown for the night. I followed the main highway, bypassing Adelaide city centre, and headed east towards Melbourne, sticking firmly to the main roads.

It was the main truck route, but still a fairly quiet road, and I was watching my rear-vision mirror constantly. Then I saw it: a green Toyota speeding up behind me. My heart stopped, and I reached for the phone, but the two young girls in the car didn't even look sideways as they raced past.

The rest of the journey was uneventful. I arrived home the next afternoon, exhausted but safe. Rod was glad to see me home safely. He didn't have to work hard to extract a promise from me never to drive to Mildura on my own again. We discussed my nightmare trip a number of times. For quite a while, I was irrationally worried about the stalkers finding my address from my registration number. Then the whole episode eventually faded, as bad dreams eventually do. It was nice to be home and feeling safe.

CHAPTER 8

ONE YEAR LATER

I had long since pushed the memory of my trip to Mildura to the back of my mind. Since that time, however, I had not ventured north of Melbourne. I'd been on another trip to South Australia, but I travelled west, on the main road through Adelaide, and gave Mildura a wide berth.

Early one morning almost twelve months after that awful day, the phone rang. Racing in from the deck, I grabbed the receiver.

"Julie!"

"Hi, Susie. How are you?"

"Julie, do you get country radio?"

"Of course not, silly; we're in the city. Why?" I asked. Susan was obviously very excited about something.

"I'm putting the phone near the radio. Can you hear it?"

"Yes … just. What's going on?"

"Listen," Susan instructed.

"Victorian police converged on Ouyen this morning, after a thirty-five-year old woman and her teenage daughter complained about a driver who stalked her …"

Feeling all the blood draining from my brain, I dropped to the floor. The room was echoing and I couldn't take any more in. The memories came flooding back as I imagined what this woman and child had endured at the hands of the stalker.

"Julie. Julie. Are you okay?"

I took a deep breath. "Yes, I'm okay. Wow, I thought I was over all that. What happened?" I was incredulous.

"At seven o'clock this morning, the woman and her daughter set off from Bendigo, heading north-west to Mildura. At Boigbeat, a man in a green car started to follow them. He did what happened to you, driving right up behind her, then dropping back, later overtaking her and slamming on the brakes so that she had to swerve to miss him. She narrowly missed a collision with a family in a four-wheel drive towing a caravan. The driver of the four-wheel drive pulled over, as did the woman with the girl." Susan sounded really concerned.

"Oh my God," I responded. "He really did exist. I wasn't imagining things."

"You still doubt what happened to you, Julie?"

I was embarrassed, as I didn't realise I'd spoken out loud. "Yeah, I still find it hard to believe all that happened."

"Well, it did happen, and it's happened again. This time it was nearly fatal. I think that you should ring Mildura police and remind them that this has happened before."

"What happened? Did they catch him this time?" I asked.

"No. While the family with the caravan was making sure that the woman and her daughter were okay, the stalker took off, and no one noticed which way he went."

"This time, though," Susan continued, "the car was a green station wagon with newspaper on the back windows and no number plates."

"Wow, that was bit cheeky, wasn't it?" I replied. "Was everyone okay?"

"Physically, yes," Susan replied. "Emotionally, they were a bit shaken, as you'd be able to relate to."

"I've been through my phone accounts and I have the date and time that you rang Mildura Police Station," Susan advised me. "I think you should call them, because they might have forgotten about the two guys who stalked you. Do you have the details?"

"Yes, it would be in my journal. I just have to look for the appropriate date."

Susan gave me the details of the date and time that she called Mildura police. I was still a bit amazed that Susan had kept all of her phone accounts in such form that she could recall a particular call on a particular date! She also gave me the phone number for Mildura Police Station. I headed off to find the journal.

A few minutes later, I rang the police.

"Good morning. Senior Constable Blamey speaking. How can I help you?"

I started to tell my story, when he interrupted me to ask if I'd mind holding while he called the duty sergeant to the phone. As I waited, I started to relive the episode of twelve months ago. It left me feeling cold.

"Good morning. Sergeant Snow speaking. My senior constable tells me that you have some information that may assist us in our enquiries. Are you able to come in to the station?"

"Not really. I live in Melbourne."

"What do you have to tell us?" he asked.

"Well, almost a year ago, you and I had a conversation about a stalker who had followed me from Winchester to Ouyen. It was exactly what happened today to the woman and her daughter."

"I vaguely remember this," he replied. "Didn't we send a car to meet you at Ouyen? You were from Melbourne and off to South Australia next."

"Yes, that's right. I have the date and time that my sister called you from Melbourne. You should have the details about the jokers who stalked me," I replied.

Providing him with as much detail as I could, I left him to his investigation. I gave him my phone number and told him to call me if he needed anything further.

About an hour later, Sergeant Snow rang me back.

"I found the report. We were lucky, because we moved into a new station on that day and I was worried that the report might have gotten lost. I'm happy to say that my officers did the right thing and filed the report. The similarities are astounding. It's a different car though; the car involved today was a station wagon," Sergeant Snow explained.

"One of the cars was a station wagon."

"There were two cars involved? Our report doesn't mention a second car." I'd caught him by surprise.

"Well, I didn't mention much about the station wagon because it joined the primary stalker much later. It was actually a blue station wagon, but they can paint cars. I believe that it had no plates and had newspaper on the rear windows."

"Yes, that's right," replied Sergeant Snow. "And you're right that they could have painted it. We've checked the plates you provided again, without any success."

Then came the words that I had not wanted to hear: "We may never catch this guy." Sergeant Snow told me, "We just have to hope that he makes a mistake. That's how we will catch him."

"Unfortunately that means he has to commit another crime," I replied.

"Yes …" said Sergeant Snow, trailing off.

I left him with that thought.

So there really was a car stalker on Highway 79 and I had escaped his clutches. He was back a year later and had chosen his next victims. It made me wonder how many women had been followed and hadn't reported the incident. Incidents like this can end very badly indeed.

They didn't find him this time either. No one could even give a description of him, and the car was untraceable. One thing was for certain: I'd never make that journey to Mildura again on my own, and if I was ever stalked again, I would not hesitate to call 0-0-0.

I'd advise you to do the same.

INTRODUCTION

Australia came through the Second World War relatively unscathed, and it boomed in the postwar period. It needed people. Thousands, from dozens of countries and speaking hundreds of languages, poured off the boats into a new country. Anyone who wanted to work had a chance: Yugoslavs, South Americans, Russians, Canadians, even Germans—anyone except the Japanese (for obvious reasons). British in particular were sought out, chosen as more likely to blend in according to the post-war "White Australia" policy. At a time when Jumbos had trunks, not wings, it took four weeks and cost a year's wage to travel from Portsmouth to Fremantle, unless you were offered a place as a "Ten-Pound Pom". The Australian government subsidised travel for fit men and their families, so a whole family could migrate for the princely sum of £10. My parents, faced with the imminent closure of the coal mines in which my father was a foreman (and delayed several times by the regular arrival of new children), "won" this "lottery" in 1966, and we arrived in August of that year.

A whole city had been built to accommodate the masses working at Holden's new car factory, and Whyalla's steel mill and shipyards were hungry for labour. Most of us ended up at one of those places.

As a small child, I always considered that the turnstiles of life swept my family through a life of dirty polluted rivers, unimaginable unemployment, and the certainty of poverty. This, had we not immigrated to Australia in the sixties, would have led to a huge decline in the way our middle-class life had treated us, at least so far. However, I never considered my real status in Australia until recently.

I wrote my story as a gift to my youngest sister, who had been born just before we left England. I realise it's lengthy, but until I read the book I have described, I hadn't realised that the "Ten-Pound Pom" wasn't considered "enough of a person" to actually have a history worth mentioning. I'm here to tell you that we did. When people read my sister's story at her fortieth birthday party, they all, without exception said, "This is my story." It was then that I realised that this wasn't just our story; this was the tale of the immigrant child, forty years on.

THE IMMIGRANT CHILD,
FORTY YEARS ON

As I shopped today for a birthday card for my youngest sister for her fortieth birthday, I realised that she was three months old when we left England on 26 July 1966. That means that I am privileged to have lived in this beautiful country, Australia, for the past forty years.

Why Did We Leave?

As a seven-year-old child, I built lasting memories of the land of my birth, Manchester, England, that included dirty air, polluted canals, and derelict housing estates. Our neighbours were being herded into high-rise apartments, and the coal mines in which my father worked were closing down. Fortunately, we left before the real brunt of those closures was felt in the burgeoning rise in unemployment.

Don't get me wrong, there were some really positive aspects to living in Manchester. We had the support of our extended family, with an abundance of grandparents, aunts, uncles and cousins. We were also very involved in the church, and we all attended the local Catholic school. We had the freedom to explore our local stomping grounds, and I know for a fact that my parents would cringe at some of the spots we visited, even though I was in the care of two older brothers.

My parents were an unlikely union at the time: my father an Irish Republican; my mother born of Protestant parents bred in England. However, I think the whole situation was made much simpler because my mother had converted to Catholicism some years before they'd met. My father was a hard-working man who provided well for his family despite his very sad and disadvantaged upbringing.

We left England with six children as "Ten-Pound Poms" and were absolutely amazed to find the streets of our neighbourhood lined with well-wishers eager to cheer us on our journey. This was a great adventure we were realising: one that most people could not even imagine embarking upon, not even in their wildest dreams. Australia was just too far away, and to leave family and friends behind was inconceivable to most. Many people had not even ventured out of Manchester in their whole lives.

The Boat Trip

After what seemed like a never-ending train journey from Manchester, we boarded the cruise ship the *Fairstar* at Southampton for what was to be the first real holiday we had ever had. Can you imagine the delight we had with four weeks of free movies, our choice of swimming pools, wonderful food, and sights we had never even heard of? We attended school every morning and learnt about decimal currency and what to expect in the way of flora and fauna in our newly adopted country, Australia. We arrived in Fremantle and then sailed on to Adelaide, arriving on my brother's tenth birthday, and felt eager to find our land legs.

Sadly, the abundant jobs my father had been led to believe existed at Holden's auto plant in Elizabeth were nonexistent. He spent many days outside the "labour exchange", waiting for something to come up. He did, however, make lasting friendships with some of the other men who also waited and searched for work.

Our Initial Impressions

In the meantime, my family lived in a migrant hostel, in ex-army Nissen huts with no air conditioning, with communal dining, and with no television or radio, but (most importantly) with no razor wire keeping us in. As children we had the freedom to explore our surroundings and made friends easily at our new schools, even if we were called "Ten-Pound Poms". It made us work very hard to adapt our speech, until in no time we looked and sounded like our fellow Aussies. We were in heaven!

My mother, I think, was often sad and lonely, with a new baby and five other children under twelve years of age to care for. She was often left alone to cope while my father went away to look for work. There were no unemployment benefits in those days, rent needed to be paid, and our meagre savings had dwindled away quickly. One of my distinct memories is of coming across my mother (always the strong one, I thought) crying inconsolably because she hadn't heard from my father in more than two weeks. Dad had travelled up to Whyalla with a mate to find work, and the rent needed to be paid by the next day. There were no phones, and certainly no mobile phones—in other words, no means of communication. If the rent wasn't paid, we would have to move out. We also wouldn't have any food. This was really serious, and we had nowhere to turn. Fortunately, Dad came through with a telegram and a money order the next day, and we survived another week.

Our Final Settlement

Dad found work in Whyalla, as a labourer in the gritty hell of the blast furnace. Mum and six children followed him, and then we celebrated our new home by adding another boy to the family. We arrived in Whyalla just in time for summer: 38–40°C for weeks at a time, when even the lucky families had only a fan. Then there was the dust: everything was permanently coated in a thick layer of red dust. There were no roads, and no supermarkets, so my mother had to drag the baby pram (backwards) three miles there and back to a small shop on the dirt road each day for supplies. The supermarket and shopping centre, along with the sealed roads that followed, were a blessing. In the meantime, did we complain? No more than any other "Pom", but I don't distinctly remember doing so. There were so many other things to give thanks for that we didn't give a second thought to the negatives. I'd had the first shower in my life on board the *Fairstar*, and in Manchester we had a tin bath in front of the fire every Saturday night. Here we had a shower *and* a bath! I know Mum didn't miss filling and emptying the tin bath for seven children!

The next shock came when we went to register the family at school, only to find that in Australia one had to pay for an education at Catholic schools, which was free in England. On a labourer's pay, it was impossible to afford to send us all to a private school, but we all had a good education. I must admit the only reason I can recall all the words to the national anthem of the day, "God Save the Queen", is because we sang it every Monday morning at assembly. (I sometimes wonder if children still sing the national anthem at school.) We were also privileged (though we didn't think it at the time) to have our times tables firmly etched in our minds by "sing-song" recital every morning of our primary school lives.

New Values

We spent our summers happily whiling away the hours, exploring, or getting sunburnt at the local swimming pool. There were games of cricket (even the girls were allowed to play) and footy on the front lawn, and when we were a little older, on the nights when it was too hot to sleep, we'd sit on the front veranda quietly talking amongst ourselves or with the neighbours. Life was simple, every day an adventure.

In Whyalla, there were two types of homes, Housing Trust and non–Housing Trust. We lived in a three-bedroom Housing Trust house and squeezed in two sets of bunks with a tiny chest of drawers in between into two of those rooms. I know I keep saying it, but it's true we were in heaven! We had a garden where fruit and vegetables grew, and we raised chickens for their fresh eggs. With this being the last house in town in those days, the bush was literally over our back fence. My brothers and I explored the bush and made cubby houses in trees, found lizards, and had a wonderful childhood. There always seemed to be a cot in my parents' room, and once the last of the babies moved in with the big kids, the mozzie-proof enclosed cot served well as a rabbit hutch for many years. We also managed to squeeze in a lodger, which helped to pay the bills. These days, my kids tell me that "just everyone" has their own room with a full-sized double bed and their own stereo to boot. How do they survive?

How Do You Settle in to a New Country?

The boys immediately embraced Australian Rules football and played for the local club. I distinctly remember a photo of their team in the local paper titled "League of Nations". From memory, there were twenty-three different nationalities between the under-twelves and under-fourteens combined; it was multiculturalism at its best! I don't think I met my first true-blue Aussie until about three years after we arrived in Australia! Initially people clung to their roots and only gradually blended in to the Australian way of life. In a small country town with lots of migrants, that was just how it happened. I guess in retrospect, it wasn't so easy for the non-English-speaking migrants, but their children and then the next generation just became "Aussies", longing more than ever to fit in. The aboriginal kids at our school came from well-respected families in the community and most excelled at sport. I can quite honestly say that I never heard a racially motivated comment levelled at any person in the whole of my school years.

I have many pleasant memories of going to cabarets with Mum and Dad and being taught to dance. The risk my parents took in throwing caution to the wind and seeking a better life for their children was enormous. I realise now my parents' sadness and longing to see family and friends. We mainly socialised with Irish and English couples in the early years. I also understand now why refugees, for instance, form enclaves: there is a sense of safety in numbers and in being valued and not judged. Everyone wants to feel that they have a sense of belonging. My parents were founding members of the Irish–Australian Association in Whyalla, which sponsored great music and dancing events and held barbecues for all the family. The girls all became "Irish dancers". Dad was a great dancer, spinning the reels with the best of them.

Finally We Became Australians

The years seem to have passed by quickly. All of my parents' seven children were honestly, gainfully, and professionally employed. Not a bad effort, I think. If we had stayed in Manchester, we would have ended up in the housing estates we see portrayed on TV dramas such as *The Bill*. How many of us would have been employed, I wonder. How many of us would have turned to drugs and crime? All but one of us has married, and there are now thirteen of the next generation, and five of the next again. My parents and most of my siblings own our own homes and live reasonably comfortable lives.

If we had stayed in England, it would have possibly been an issue that none of us married other Catholics. I am married to an atheist, my other siblings to various other denominations. My youngest sister married a Greek man, in the Greek Orthodox Church to keep his parents happy. They did, however, have their marriage vows renewed the next day in the Catholic church, because they didn't feel married, not having been able to understand the Greek Orthodox service! My parents said that we should marry whom we loved and who loved us and placed no restrictions on us. It is interesting, though, that of all of us, I am the only one who educated my children in the Catholic system and my children are the only ones to have made all of their sacraments. Laziness? No, I think it was simply that they had a choice and they made it. It was more important to me, so I followed my own choice. My children now make their own choices and don't attend church and may decide not to educate their children in the Catholic system. That's the beauty of living in Australia; we can make our own choices. In England we would all have educated our children in the Catholic system, as it would have been expected.

I love my country. I am a naturalised Australian and totally proud of it. I feel a great sense of pride when I hear the national anthem or when I see a great Aussie achievement on TV, or anywhere for that matter. My heart swells and my eyes tear up. I support Australia first and foremost in all of our sporting, political, and other challenges. Last year, on my first trip to the UK since I left there, I travelled on my Aussie passport to England, Ireland, and France, and came home very glad that I live in this wonderful country, Australia. We really do live in the best country in the world.

Yes, there are issues in our country which need to be addressed.

The public health system is sadly lacking in some areas, and I find it very sad, and totally inappropriate, that the sick and the elderly are placed on such long waiting lists for surgery and the like. The elderly, after all, created the lifeblood of this country, but they are cast off so easily in what should be their golden years. This is particularly evident in isolated regions.

My biggest concern of all is the mental health issue, particularly in the public sector, where I am appalled at the treatment, or lack of it, and the condition of the various psychiatric units. The poor care of our mentally ill has led to homelessness and incarceration in many cases. The deinstitutionalisation of many severely intellectually disabled people in recent years has seen homelessness increase, and many people inappropriately housed and at risk. The number of homeless people is rising at an alarming rate, and there is a great shortage of affordable rental housing.

Forty Years On

Still, forty years on, I am happy that I can walk down my street and not have to worry too much about being mugged or shot at. The likelihood that I will be in a building bombed by terrorists is low. I am not in this lifetime likely to have to be worried about atrocities carried out by invading soldiers or civil war. The pollution levels are not likely in my lifetime to be so bad that I can't enjoy a sunny Melbourne day. Our rivers and reservoirs are clean and monitored, and I have an adequate supply of clean drinking water. I am not likely ever to starve to death due to lack of food supplies. My husband and I own property and cars, we have jobs and finances for goods and services, clothing, and fine dining. There are cinemas, good books to read, excellent libraries, and public services. Private health services are readily available to us, and there are excellent private hospitals to choose from. My children have been well educated, and there are good, well-paying jobs available. I can hop on a plane, on one of the safest airlines in the world, to see my family and friends and be with them in an hour, even though I live so far away from them. I am unlikely ever to experience the devastation of tsunamis, landslides, or hurricanes in my country. I can find employment easily and can expect to be treated fairly in the workplace. Freedom of expression is encouraged as we live in a democratic society. I can expect to be protected and governed by our laws, and I know that they are in place to keep me and my fellow Australians safe. I can make my own choices within Australian law, and follow my own religious beliefs as long as they do not interfere with the rights and safety of others.

Life is good—for my parents, my family, and my fellow Australians. I have a lot to give thanks for forty years on!

POPPING THE QUESTION,
WITH A DIFFERENCE

Mark had rung this morning and sounded as though he had something special on his mind.

We'd been seeing each other for over two years now and things were getting kind of serious. Yet I didn't really know anything about him. I had no idea where he came from or what his family background was. In fact, I knew nothing other than what I had seen over the past two years. I had asked him, of course, but he always fobbed me off or changed the subject and led me down a different path. So tonight could be the night. *Maybe he's going to introduce me to his family. Or maybe he's going to propose. Oh my God, he's going to propose, That's probably it.*

I was getting more excited as the day progressed. *Oh, Juliette, I* thought, *give yourself a break. He's probably going to tell you he can't see you anymore!*

We haven't actually been fully intimate as yet, which was difficult at first. Then after I got used to the idea that he was saving it for marriage one day, I found it to be quite cute.

I tried to get through some of the paperwork on my desk, but my thoughts kept drifting back to Mark and whatever it was he was going to tell me tonight.

At 3.30 I decide to use my "early minute" for the week and head off to Genie, my favourite hairdresser, who knows exactly what to do to make my hair look fantastic. Roxanne was booked to gel my nails afterwards.

"What's the occasion?" Genie inquired.

"I'm not sure, actually. Mark has asked me on a special date tonight, and I don't really know what to expect," I replied.

"A ring!" Genie and Roxanne chorused.

"Oh, I doubt it." I reddened. I didn't want to prematurely think about a ring, and I didn't want the women guessing that he might ask me to marry him. "We'll see." I was clearly evasive, and changed the conversation to the new diet that we were all trying.

I left the salon feeling like a million dollars. I was very excited, so I decided to soak in the bath for half an hour. It wouldn't affect my new hairstyle. But I was so restless in the bath that I was in for only ten minutes or so, before I hopped out to get ready for my date. I laid out my favourite lingerie on the bed: a lovely black bra and matching panties, a garter belt with silk stockings, and an under slip. Reaching into my special wardrobe, I selected a slinky black number which hugged my figure nicely. It also helped that it was one of Mark's favourites.

A dab of Coco Chanel behind the ears; I knew Mark could never resist. A touch of lipstick completed my make-up.

Mark arrived shortly afterwards, and we headed off to our favourite French restaurant, Franc-nuit. He looked so handsome in his navy jumper, which highlighted his blond hair and blue piercing eyes.

No sooner had we sat down than Mark started to talk about our relationship and how we had become quite close to each other. He was really nervous, so I took his hand and said, "It's okay, Mark. I know there are things we need to talk about, and it's all fine. I know what you are going to say."

"You do?" Mark asked, horrified.

I was getting quite confused, so I suggested that he just come out with it. The suspense was killing me.

"I know we've grown closer over the past twelve months," Mark started, "and I'd like us to get closer still." I smiled a knowing smile. "But I'm in a witness protection program, indefinitely, and I need to move on. I'd like you to come with me."

I just sat there with my mouth open. He had fooled me completely; I never would have guessed he was in witness protection. I had to make a decision.

"Wow, Mark, that's a lot to digest all at once," I exclaimed. "It's really exciting, but scary too. I really need to think about this."

Mark looked at me with so much love in his eyes. "I know I have a lot to explain, but just remember, I'm a good person. Just because I'm in witness protection doesn't necessarily mean that I have done something wrong. I just need protection. And I think that if you and I are to make this relationship permanent, you will need protection too."

We both became very quiet and thoughtful. There was a lot to consider.

"Well, I guess we should go somewhere private to discuss where we go from here," I suggested.

"Yes, I agree," replied Mark, still wearing that loving smile. "Your place or mine? *Garcon, l'addition, s'il vous plait!*"

WHAT DO YOU SEE WHEN
YOU LOOK AT ME?

What do you see when you look at me, Mummy? Can you see further than my blond hair and big blue eyes? Can you see the little boy trapped deep inside?

I know that my shouting hurts your head, Mummy. You don't always understand what I want when I flap my hands, run in circles, and make loud noises. But you have Daddy to talk to, and I'm so alone.

When I can't sleep for most of the night, Mummy, I know the whole family is awake too and that you are all exhausted. Do you ever wonder if I am tired too?

You send me to "program" to give you respite from my noises, my strange movements, and my wet nappies. Do you ever think that I would like a break from this too?

Look into my eyes, Mummy. I know it is difficult, because my eyes look everywhere but at you. But what do you see—a word, a diagnosis, or a little boy trapped inside, alone and afraid?

I know I have autism, Mummy. You and Daddy often talk about it with the doctors at the big hospital.

They say that I will never speak, but how do they know, Mummy? I have words and sounds locked away, deep inside. I practise them every day, but to you they are just noises.

Mummy, I know that you're tired. I know you're sad and I know you're frustrated. But please, remember that I'm just a little boy, Mummy, trapped inside a lonely, empty world. And one day I'd like to come out to play with you.

AUTISM

White hair, big blue eyes.
Nothing seems amiss at first.
Tell-tale cracks appear.
Milestones never reached, blank look,
Eye contact fails, empty mind.

FLICKERING

Flames flicker in the hearth.
Hearth is built of solid stone.
Stone house withstands the storm.
Storm flashes streaks of lightning.

Lightning frightens our canine friends.
Friends huddle around the fire.
Fire provides us with warmth.
Warmth is missed in winter.

Winter sees us chilled to the bone.
Bone-weary after chopping.
Chopping wood to feed the flames.
Flames flicker in the hearth.

WHERE THE OUTBACK MEETS THE SEA

Where the outback meets the sea,
The blue line prominent on a crisp spring day.
White sand rushes to meet the sea
As it curves in an arc away from the shore.

Seaweed lingers on the foreshore, and
Play equipment swings lazily alone in the sun.
Norfolk Island palms towering over the gardens
As dolphins pop up to say hello in the marina.

Heading out of town and the greenery fades.
Saltbush and straggly trees adorn the landscape.
Huge pipeline runs alongside the road,
Gushing water to keep the town alive.

The steel monsters spew out steam,
And the noisy machinery breaks the silence.
A highway leading to wherever you want to go;
And you always return.

It's in the blood, this ragged town,
Like a magnet drawing us back time and time again.
But like the steel monsters,
We will one day cease to come.

One less visitor to the town …
Where the outback meets the sea.

THE TOOTH THIEF

I'll tell a tale of dentistry.
'Twas more a case of butchery.
Old Doctor Gill was a quack—
Really should've been given the sack.

"Open very wide," he'd say,
And with this we'd start to pray.
In he went with all his tools;
Out he came with all our jewels.

Why wouldn't he just fill our teeth?
He behaved just like a tooth thief.
All we wanted was a filling;
All he wanted was the billing.

Before too long he'd surely taken
Most teeth in town. I'm not mistaken.
People were walking 'round toothless.
Not attractive, I must confess.

The people thought they'd better act fast;
What teeth they had could be their last.
Invited the dentist to dinner one night,
But he didn't go without a fight.

They trussed him up with open smile,
Poured in a solution—'twas quite vile.
He struggled a moment then went still.
He's buried now on Primrose Hill.

A new dentist the town did find,
A better man of sounder mind.
He checks their teeth and gives a bill,
But unlike Dr Gill he'd rather fill.

The secret of old Gill's demise
Was locked away, as you might surmise.
A new business, though, on the town map:
Dentures for cheap to bridge the gap!

CAPTAIN SWEATPANTS

Well another disastrous date last night, thought James Band. Silvana was obviously a gold digger with her sights set on his money. *How can people ask how many cars I own, or blatantly ask the value of my mansions?* It was just so vulgar.

He was still smarting from his lengthy relationship with Rebecca. He'd really thought that she was the one. However, after moving in with him on trial, premarriage, she was found to be stealing and selling off his antiques. James was devastated and thought he may never date again.

He rang his good friend Lenny. Maybe Lenny could save his future, or at the very least his social life.

Lenny was free for lunch. As James described the latest experience to his friend, Lenny laughed.

"What's so funny?" James asked sulkily.

"No, it's not funny, James," replied Lenny. "It's just that I may have a solution. It may not draw in women, but it should provide the anonymity you desire."

"I'm all ears," remarked James.

Lenny had given this dilemma some thought. Even he could see that when James went into public, women threw themselves at him, and how problematic this could be. James was rich, handsome, and charming; what was not to like? But James's ability to form long-term relationships was affected as a result. Was it the money or the person these women wanted? In the beginning, having a new woman every night was fun for

James, and he was on cloud nine most of the time, but such was not the case now.

"Okay," said Lenny, "let's go for a drive."

"Where to?" James was curious.

"You'll see." Lenny smiled.

They hailed a cab and Lenny directed it to a local Goodwill store.

"What the …?"

"Be patient."

"Okay," agreed James.

Inside the store, Lenny headed for the men's trouser section, and grabbed a red toboggan hat off a shelf.

Rummaging through the racks, Lenny finally came up with a pair of blue and white chequered gym pants, which seemed to satisfy his requirements. "Try them on, James," he encouraged.

"What, me, wear these disgusting old clothes?" wailed James. "I'll never be seen in public …" Then he smiled, finally catching onto Lenny's plan.

James tugged the old gym pants up to his armpits. They both laughed. Next came the bright red toboggan hat and a pair of black horn-rimmed glasses that Lenny had also scored. "Wow."

From that time on, when it was convenient to be incognito, James wore his "disguise", and before long earned himself the title "Captain Sweatpants". Other guys thought he was a bit of a nerd around the comic book store or the supermarket, or anywhere really.

James doubted that he would ever find a woman who could see beyond his fashion faux pas. In the meantime, however, he could wander around the store and any other place he so chose incognito, not as James Band but as daggy old Captain Sweatpants—and he couldn't have been happier. Now please don't tell anyone, okay?!

LONELINESS

A void that cannot be filled,
An echo that doesn't bounce back,
A blackness that cannot be penetrated,
A bleakness that has no future.

An epidemic,
Sightless,
Soundless,
Inviting early death.

WINTER IS COMING

Winter is coming.
Winter is here.
Snow creatures running,
Creating great fear.

They cannot be killed,
For they're already dead.
With swords they are skilled,
And the people feel dread.

People ask, "What's that stone
We've heard will destroy?"
"It's magic glass honed
into blades!" I reply.

Snow creatures don't know
We have weapons to kill.
They expect sword and bow
When we meet on the hill.

Our blacksmiths have laboured
Day and night, night and day,
And the magic glass favoured
Is a blade made for affray.

Which way it will go
Is anyone's guess.
We reap what we sow
I must confess.

So who will it be
That wins the steel throne?
The dead or the living,
The winners alone.

Who will finally rise
from the fire and the dark?
'Tis not a surprise,
It will be the house Zark.

WE WON!

We were sitting down to watch the evening movie when the lottery results came on the screen. "Twenty-two ... thirteen ... eight ... thirty ... four."

"Oh my God!" I squealed. "I have five numbers in the lottery. I can't believe they would take an ad break just at this crucial ..."

"It gives me much pleasure to draw the final number in tonight's lottery, which has a first prize of eight hundred and eighty-eight million dollars."

"Just get on with it!" I said impatiently.

"This is the largest lottery ever drawn in Australia to date."

"Come on ..."

"And this is the last number ..."

"I need a twelve ..."

"It is number twelve. Good luck to all entrants, and I wish you a happy future. If the win is shared, each ticket holder will receive an equal share."

I could barely hear a word. There was a kind of ringing/swooshing noise in my head. My face, I could feel, was red and hot. I was shaking.

"Oh my God, I've won. Oh my God, I'm rich. It can't be right; I must have made a mistake."

Then the phone rang.

Who can that be? I wondered. I still felt like I was drifting through some kind of dream.

It was the team from Lottery Australia. I struggled to speak, managing a weak "hello". I snapped out of my fog as I realised I wasn't hearing anything the caller was saying.

"I just want to explain the results of the lottery and then leave you to your celebrations. Is that okay?"

I nodded, then realised that I needed to answer verbally. "Yes, of course."

"Four winners shared in tonight's lottery, so you'll have an equal share, okay?"

I nodded again. I was feeling a bit faint.

"Two hundred and twenty-two million dollars each …"

Yes, it was true, the cheque that was hand-delivered to me the next morning was written out in my name, for two hundred and twenty-two million dollars! It was a dream come true. Never had I thought that I'd be faced with these choices. We were battlers, worked hard all our lives, raised five children. We had never owned our own home, nor had we ever taken a holiday.

We banked the cheque and then Bruce and I sat down to plan what we would do with the money. Wanting our children to have what we'd never had, we decided to buy each of them a new home. Plus, each child would receive a million dollars.

Crikey, I thought, *that five million dollars hasn't even made a dent in our riches.* We swore that winning the lottery wouldn't change our lives, that we would stay true to the people we were, so we went out and bought a big flashy house with a swimming pool, a sauna, a gym, and most importantly, maid's quarters. I intended never to wash another dish.

The next thing on the list was that holiday, the holiday that we had always wanted but never had the money to take it. So we gathered the family together, our children and their partners and the grandchildren, and we hired a jet. What's another one and a half million dollars between friends?

We started in Rome, and were startled by the beauty of Vatican City and how much history there was on show. By contrast, Australia is a relatively new country, settled by Europeans only two hundred years ago.

Next, we visited Venice and enjoyed the gondola trip I'd always wanted. We finished off Italy and started focussing on the rest of Europe.

By now the boys were starting to get on each others' nerves. Most took their wives and families and went home.

We were touring through England and Wales when I'd finally had enough and my husband and I parted ways. I gave him one million dollars and continued on my way. I loved England, Wales, and Ireland too. But I knew I'd settle in England. I had a British passport from my childhood, and it was easily renewed.

Searching through real estate in Torquay, I finally decided on a five-acre property. A farmer grazed his sheep on my land, and I had a gardener to ensure that I had fresh fruit and vegetables.

One unseasonably warm day reminded me of Australia; of the house and family I had left behind. *What am I doing here? I've left my family on the other side of the world. I've spent half my winnings. Am I happy? Not really.*

I had done what I said I wasn't going to do: I'd let my fortune change my life completely.

"Lucy, it's Mum. I'm coming home."

JAMES, THE COGNAC, AND THE WARDROBE.

James Canning (known affectionately as JC) and Amy lived on a five-acre farm out at Twelve Mile Creek in the eighties. It had turkeys, chooks, pigs, and a greyhound or two. The youngsters used to love finding rotten turkey eggs and throwing them at each other, their aim becoming more accurate with the passage of time! Needless to say, at the end of each day (and sometimes in between), it meant a bath for whoever got smashed with rotten turkey eggs.

Getting back to JC: There were some great parties at the Canning farm. The littlies were safely amused, and the adults (some of them) often partook in a great barbeque, washed down with plenty of beer. As the day progressed, JC was getting more and more inebriated. It was always obvious that he had almost taken his fill when he started on the cognac. JC liked his cognacs and always bought the best quality. When he broke it open after a day of drinking, most of the family and friends had drifted away home. It was only the stayers who shared JC's quality nightcap.

The problem was that after a couple of glasses of cognac, JC would disappear. The first time, Amy worried about him. No one knew where he was, and a search party armed with torches fanned out across the block looking for him. We were all getting quite worried by now: it had been hours since anyone had seen him. We checked the pigpen to make sure he hadn't fallen in and become the pigs' feast for the day. Thankfully he wasn't there.

It was late and getting cold. Amy went to the wardrobe in their bedroom to get a jacket. It was a big built-in wardrobe from floor to ceiling and quite deep. When she slid open the door, she jumped and gave a little squeal, which bought everyone running. There at the bottom of the wardrobe with pillow and blanket, fast asleep, was JC.

That set a precedent. If there was a party or a barbecue that went on into the evening, after a few beers and a couple of cognacs, it would be a dead cert that you would find JC in

Narnia!

DEPLOYMENT

The scene is set in the lounge room of the home of Sylvia and Jeff Fenton. They are twenty-eight and thirty years old respectively. Their two children are Eddie, aged two, and Maria, aged five. Jeff is a US Marine and has been deployed to Afghanistan. He leaves the next morning, and his tour of duty is expected to be six months.

Tonight they have taken the children to see their grandparents Gail and Tom. Jeff's younger brother Arnie is there with his wife Julie and their two boys, Billy and Ned.

Once they arrive home, they put the children to bed after a cuddle and a story. Both children say a prayer for God to keep their daddy safe and bring him home to them in six months' time, happy and healthy.

Jeff: "This is the bit I hate." He and his wife are huddled together on the sofa. They don't seem to get close enough to each other.

Sylvia, quietly. "Me too. It's like we are saying goodbye forever."

Jeff: "I hate it when you say that, Syl. It's like you're creating bad luck."

Sylvia: "You know what I mean. It's the uncertainty and the anticipation of loss when you're away and that uncomfortable period when you get home and can't or won't talk about your time away. I know you see and do awful things, but you're just doing your job."

Jeff, smirking: "Just doing my job? I shot a boy not much older than Maria on my last tour. How do I cope with that?"

Sylvia, hugging Jeff close: "I know that's really tough, but he had an explosive device strapped to him. It was either him or you and twenty of your guys!"

Jeff: "Yeah, I know. But it haunts me, Syl. Sometimes, just when I'm drifting off to sleep, I can see his face, those white teeth against his tanned skin … Then he just kind of bursts and I'm covered in blood and bones and grey matter. I can make out some of his white teeth on the ground. It's like they're smiling at me, mocking me. I wake up sweating all over, and it's so hard to get back to sleep afterwards."

Sylvia, sadly: "Are the dreams lessening?"

Jeff: "Not really. Since I found out I'm leaving for another tour of duty, the dreams have become more and more vivid. Sometimes I feel like I'm going to explode myself."

Sylvia: "Are you still seeing the therapist?"

Jeff: "Not often. What good is it? She can't make it go away. It happened. That's all there is to it. I have to learn to deal with it."

Sylvia: "Easier said than done. Just don't let it affect your safety. When these children are sent out by their families with bombs strapped to their tiny bodies, their deaths are a sealed deal. It's not your fault, but the fault of those people who strap the bombs on and sacrifice their children's lives. I don't understand it and never will."

Jeff, shaking his head: "It's a different world out there. I could no more imagine strapping a bomb to Maria or Eddie than fly to the moon. I'll never understand it."

Sylvia: "Come on, this is our last night together for six months, and here we are talking about suicide bombers. Carry me to bed, Superman!"

They both give a quiet chuckle. Jeff, standing up, bends over to pick up his bride. He carries her tiny body into the bedroom.

It is something that has always fascinated him, how this four foot six inch, ninety-pound princess fits against his six foot six, two-hundred-fifty-pound frame. He does feel a bit like Superman sometimes.

Jeff lays Sylvia on their bed and proceeds to kiss her passionately. Then he stops: it is an unspoken given that they don't make love the night before he is deployed. It is too desperate and would make their emotions, already raw, go into overdrive.

Instead he pulls the blanket up to her chin, kisses the tip of her nose, and climbs in beside her.

They spoon together, Jeff holding her as tightly as possible without causing physical damage. He can feel the familiarity in the embrace where each part of their bodies connect. They start to drift off to sleep.

Jeff: "Love you, honey."

Sylvia: "Love you too, Superman!"

They both laugh a short sad laugh, and cling to each other in an embrace.

Jeff settles into a restless sleep.

Jeff: "No ... no ... go back inside the house ... I don't want to hurt you ... No ... no ... nooooooooooo!"

It is the young boy again, smiling, white teeth, tanned skin, black hair, red jumper, and a vest strapped onto his little body. He holds his arm out to the side, with a wire attached to the vest and what appears to be a switch in his hand.

Jeff is in the middle of a war zone in his dream, tossing and turning, his breathing ragged. Then suddenly he bolts upright. His breathing calms as he realises he is still at home in his own bed, with his darling Sylvia, who is sitting upright too, staring into his eyes with concern.

Sylvia: "Was it the same dream? With the boy?"

Jeff, catching his breath: "Yeah ... Oh God, Sylvia, what if I'm faced with the same situation this tour? I don't think I could kill another kid!"

Sylvia: "Try not to dwell on it. I know that's easier said than done, but you need your sleep. Do you want me to put on some relaxation tapes?"

Jeff: "Yeah, that sometimes helps. Jeez, Syl, I'm so sorry to worry you like this, but I just can't seem to stop the dreams from coming."

Sylvia: "It's okay, Jeff. Just relax and listen to the music. Let's see if you can salvage a bit more sleep tonight."

Jeff: "Did I tell you how much I love you?"

Sylvia: "Yes, every day. I'm the luckiest woman alive. Just sleep, and you'll head off tomorrow and be back before we know it."

They both drift back to a restless sleep. Next thing they know, it is six in the morning and the alarm is blaring.

Jeff jumps out of bed and heads for the shower. Sylvia goes in to rouse the children. They do everything by rote on the days when Jeff leaves for his tour of duty. Even young Eddie seems to know that something is happening and needs lots of cuddles.

They eat breakfast in relative silence and then pile into the car for the trip to the deployment base.

Eddie: "Daddy going away?"

Jeff, struggling with his emotions: "Yes, buddy, but I'll be home before you know it."

Maria: "I remember last time you went away, Daddy. It seemed like you were away for years."

Jeff, laughing: "Well, it wasn't years, honey. Daddy was away for six months, and I'll be away for the same time this tour too. I'll be hurrying home to you both."

They arrive at the base. All of the other marines are ready to board the bus which will take them to the plane. Families gather around. Tears are shed, but people try to keep their emotions in check so as not to upset the younger children.

Jeff, to the children: "I'll write to you both, and I hope to see some letters and drawings from you, okay? Mind your mother, and help as much as you can. Mommy will be writing to me every week, so I'll know whether you've been good or not!"

Sylvia: "I know that they will be good children, Daddy. You just go and don't worry about us. Just keep safe and write often."

Jeff, saluting to his son: "Be good, buddy. Love you and see you soon. Give Daddy a hug."

He turns to Maria and gave her a hug and kiss too.

Jeff: "Love you, sweetheart. Look out for your brother and mind your Mommy, okay?"

Jeff and Sylvia cling together, neither wanting to let go first. Eventually he has to tear himself away, kissing Sylvia passionately, and then holding her apart from him as if to commit her to memory. Neither can say anything, as usual. Parting is too painful. And if they say anything, they will become too emotional and the children will pick up on it.

One last hug and he is off.

Jeff: "I love you, Syl."

Sylvia: "Love you too, honey. Stay safe."

Then the marines board the bus and they are gone. Sylvia feels a bit lost. She speaks to a few of the other wives and then loads the children into the car, ready for the short drive home.

The next week is a blur, and then Sylvia starts to get a bit restless. Waiting for that first letter home always makes her antsy. She looks out to the letterbox and sees that there is mail.

She runs out excitedly to check to see who it is from.

No letter!

The next day is the same—no letter. This is unusual, but then sometimes the soldiers are preoccupied and away from the base, and it takes longer to get that first letter home.

The next day there is the eagerly awaited letter. It is brief.

Hi, honey. Hope you are all well. We've been dug in for a few
days and things have been pretty hectic. We're okay, so don't
worry. Give the kids a big hug and kiss from me. I love you,
honey, and miss you.
All my love,
Jeff xxxxxx

Sylvia has mixed feelings, but she is glad to receive a letter, no matter
how brief. Perhaps she and the kids could put together a care package
this afternoon. Families often send them over, to help the marines with
the isolation and homesickness they feel.

There is a knock on the door.

Sylvia, calling out: "I'm coming. I'll just be a minute." She scoops
Eddie up and, holding him on her hip, walks quickly to the front door.
Then she slows. Through the glass she can see two figures in uniform.
Her brain becomes cloudy with confusion.

Sylvia opens the front door with trepidation.

Officer, quietly: "Good morning, Mrs Fenton. I'm Colonel Mark
Duvall, and this is Father Paul Wilson. May we please come in?"

Sylvia almost drops Eddie. She can't speak, but motions for them to
come inside. She feels lightheaded and almost as if she is up on the ceiling,
watching herself and the officers down below. Her head is buzzing and
she can't take in what is being said.

Colonel: "Sorry to have … on a mission … young boy … explosive …
detonated in a crowd …"

Sylvia: "Nooooooooooooooooooooo!"

Sylvia falls to the floor, a mess of emotions, grief, disbelief, denial.

Sylvia: "Oh my God, it actually happened!"

DEPRESSION

Dark and gloomy are the thoughts
Echoing into my brain,
Punishing me for my deeds,
Resonating inside my skull.
Eclectic, dissociative, intrusive,
Shades of black, shades of grey,
Swimming through treacle,
Invading my life.
Omnipresent and changeable,
Never ending, never subsiding, never free.

BIPOLARITY

Bursting, thrusting through my brain,
Images impossible to contain.
Private is my inner blow.
Only the closest to me know.
Labile, laughing, low then high
Is just part of nature's lie.
Reveals an empty inner soul.
Mania in a mixing bowl.
Obsessively following rituals.
Overtly revealing habituals.
Doona-diving follows suit.
Depression as a word is moot.
Invisible voices, noises call,
Swinging like a wrecking ball.
Oh how I wish it would all stop.
Rebounding from the depths to the top.
Disorder teasing sanity.
Ever-changing symmetry
Revealing fears of insanity.

ALZHEIMER'S—LOCKED INSIDE

It was a sad day indeed when the confusion came to stay, and likewise,

Likewise the fear of what was yet to come. I felt zapped,

Zapped, as I watched the illness steal away

your dignity, and I felt helpless,

Helpless, as you were reduced to a child who could speak,

Speak but not comprehend, those blue eyes—

Eyes—staring at me vacantly, leading me to tears, while I watched,

Watched, your shattered pride, with the loss,

Loss of control of your bodily functions … My God,

My God, the end would be a blessing. Erstwhile.

Erstwhile a man strong and true, he had been robbed,

Robbed, of the dignity he once had, so now sleep.

Sleep the eternal sleep, Daddy, and may God bless you.

God bless you and pass you in to the arms of a mother you never knew.

DISORDERLY ORDER OF THE MIND

Today I am calm and serene.
Tomorrow I'm caught in between.
Now a rusty spring tightly coiled;
Next a spring lightly oiled.

My mind is full to overflowing.
Thoughts and feelings now are growing.
Too many images in my head.
Defragmentation fills me with dread.

Where will my thoughts go today?
Will I remember this affray?
Why does nature allow this torture,
Create a mind that submits to disorder?

"I want to be normal!" I cry,
Offering my face to the sky,
Yet I know that peace will never occur.
I am destined for calamity to recur.

Through my life I've learnt to hide
The emotions I battle with inside.
No one would guess my inner struggle
Attached to my core like a shackle.

Lonely I wander through life,
Ne'er revealing my constant strife.
I learn to control my private turmoil,
Not allowing my mind to publicly uncoil.

75

For if I do, people may judge,
And my need to seem normal won't budge.
Will I ever be free from this pain
Emanating from my tired brain?
I think not!

THE LONE PIPER

A lonely figure silhouetted against the night sky.
Kilted in his battalion's tartan and long wooden socks,
He stands proudly, for a moment, at his post,
Lovingly caressing his bagpipes, fingering the pipes.

Crafted from a small sheep, the legs are attached to the bone pipes.
He fills the bag with a huge breath, continually, creating the basic note.
Cheeks puffed out fully as he raises the pipe to his lips.
A mournful sound pierces the night's silence.

The music tells the tale of their battle,
A battle that has been fought and won.
The piper signalling day's end, recognising the courage of the men.
The music tells the men to rest now and resume on the morrow.

But this battle is over and has been won that very day.
The lone piper tells the tale
Of how the battle commenced with courage and vigour,
How his compatriots fought gallantly and defeated the enemy.
And now they rest to count their dead and nurse their wounded.
There is time to mourn a friend from childhood
Who travelled on a boat to this stark land.
Together they fought the battle in their minds,

Before being sent over the top separately.
'Twas he who found his unfortunate friend
Bleeding profusely in a pool of mud.
No time to turn to drag him to safety.

It would have been too late in any case.
He wonders how he will face the parents,
If he is lucky enough to return home one day himself.
He listens to the wild refrains of the lone piper.

It makes him feel safe for now …
Tomorrow is another day!

I'M NOT PERFECT

I'm not perfect, but I'd like to be.
If I were perfect, I'd make great tea.
My cuppa skills I can't guarantee.
So no, I'm not perfect, but I'd like to be.

I'm no expert, but I'd like to be.
I'd give great advice on making tea.
People would queue cos they love great tea.
But I'm not as perfect as I'd like to be.

I'm not the best at making tea.
I've been told by experts, you see.
It's either too milky or weak as pee.
So I'm not perfect, but I'd like to be.

If I were to brew us a pot of tea,
It probably would fail to be
The best pot of tea you'd ever see,
Cos I'm not perfect but I'd like to be.

I'm not a genius at making tea,
But what should great tea aim to be?
Dark and fragrant or light like chi?
If I knew I'd be perfect, as I'd like to be.

I'm not perfect, but I'd like to be.
I'd like to make the perfect tea
That everyone would drink with me.
If not I'd be happy, cos I could see

That if you want a decent drink at my place, you should choose coffee!

PW THE EXTORTIONIST

I was fourteen years old and our parents were quite strict. My friend Sally and I were offered a lift home on a motorbike, ridden by Sally's brother David and his friend Greg. We had been at the fete at the local primary school, when we met up with them and they offered us a ride. I knew that our parents wouldn't approve, so I asked David to drop me at the corner of our street.

As luck would have it, who should be coming round the corner at that very moment but my older brother PW? Now Paul was a fink, without a doubt, and if he could a manipulate a situation into his favour, then he would. So for the next two weeks, poor me, I was to do his bidding. He blackmailed me. I had no choice but to comply. He would say, "Make me a cup of tea," and I would say, "Make your own tea." He would quietly call, "Muuuuuuuuuuum!" I would just jump up and do as I was asked. He would say, "Iron my shirt," "Make me some toast," "Polish my shoes," and I would just have to suck it up.

This lasted two weeks, until I broke. Poor little old me, I just couldn't take it any longer. So I ran to our mum and told her the whole story, about the motorbike, about how PW had seen me and blackmailed for the past two weeks, and how I just couldn't take it any longer.

Mum sat and listened and was very quiet. I thought she was probably calculating an appropriate punishment. To my surprise she burst out laughing: "Dear, I think you've been punished enough!"

PW lost his slave!

ALIEN INVASION

Jamie's vantage point gave him a clear view of the events unfolding down below the embankment. Lying belly down, he peeked through the long grass. The hairs on the back of his neck stood up. Jamie was fourteen years of age and should have been at school; however, curiosity about the stories surrounding the spaceships was just too much for this inquisitive boy to bear.

For the past week, the rumour mill had been working overtime, with stories of aliens and scorch marks on the fields of corn and wheat. No one had a feasible explanation.

Wow, thought Jamie, *I have a ringside seat.*

From where he lay, he observed the tall stringy beings. They were iridescent purple in colour, with long giraffe-like necks. There were no eyes as far as Jaime could tell, but each had an antenna which appeared to aid its mobility.

"Oh, crikey," Jamie exclaimed. "They have little kids; I wonder what they are going to do with them." The children seemed to be hypnotised and were walking two abreast, holding hands, towards the aliens' massive spaceship.

He shook his head as if to clear his vision, and pinched himself to see if he was dreaming. "Ouch, nope, not dreaming!"

Jamie realised that he had better get help, and started crawling backwards commando-style towards his bike. He realised that there was a hovering sound above him, which was growing louder and louder.

"What the? … Noooooooooo! Leave me alone!" cried Jamie. "Let me go."

But it was too late. The beings had detected him, hiding on the top of the hill in the long grass, and decided that he would be specimen 97. Jamie was one of the few in good condition: almost all the children had medical conditions and needed regular medication. Some had minor birth defects that the mothers had worried about all their lives; these had been chosen by the aliens for the variety.

Silently Jamie was levitated by the pointy finger of a purple being and floated down towards the queue of children, entering the alien vessel. There was no time for Jamie to ponder his future. His thoughts were now under the control of his captors.

The last of the children was loaded on board, followed in by the remaining purple custodians, and the mammoth doors closed behind them.

Within thirty seconds the great ship had risen upwards and jetted away at phenomenal speed, unwitnessed by human eyes.

Or so they thought.

True Colours

Paul Barry was also fourteen years of age. He had recently undergone surgery to place rods in his fractured spine, following a motor vehicle accident, in which he was a passenger. The car had collided with a semitrailer at considerable speed. Paul spent three months in an induced coma while his brain recovered from the impact of the collision. He had suffered a subdural haematoma and needed burr-hole surgery to relieve the pressure and remove the blood clot from his temporal lobe.

While Paul was comatose, it was unknown whether the damage to his brain was permanent and would affect his hearing and the ability to process the information he heard, translating into meaningful speech and words. In addition to this, Paul had sustained crush fractures to his eleventh and twelfth thoracic vertebrae. He had undergone decompression surgery to relieve pressure on the spinal cord. It was unknown whether he would walk again or even regain the use of his legs. However, the good news was that the swelling around the nerves was slowly subsiding.

Paul had awoken from his coma only seven days previously and was spending his days in various positions on a tilted bed, which changed his position to avoid pressure sores. In addition to this, the change of position assisted with digestion and allowed him to read more comfortably and to watch television.

The good news that day was that the latest tests showed no permanent damage to the brain. The swelling was subsiding, and his language, hearing, and sequencing skills were almost back to normal.

While Paul was recovering, he was using his father's telescope to view the surrounding areas of the rehabilitation centre.

Yesterday, he had thought that he'd seen some sort of flying saucer in the sky, around dusk, but he immediately dismissed it.

He didn't believe in alien beings and thought that it was probably a low-flying aeroplane or something similar.

Today, however, a shocked Paul had just viewed the mass abduction of around one hundred kids, by purple creatures that loaded them into some kind of vessel and then whisked them away. The whole process had taken only ten minutes or so, and at first he didn't realise what he was viewing through the telescope. It wasn't until they snatched up the last boy and dragged him away too that Paul realised that these children may never be seen again.

He buzzed the nurse, once, twice, three times. Nurse Callahan flew down the corridor, convinced that some sort of emergency was occurring!

"Paul, Paul, what's happening?" she asked shakily.

"Space … kids … flying … flying saucers."

Oh damn, he thought, *my speech is still jumbled.*

"Calm down, Paul," soothed Nurse Callahan. "Calm down and tell me."

"Purple creatures … took heaps … kids … maybe more than a hundred … space chips."

"Oh, I see." Nurse Callahan regarded him with pity. "Yes, we get a lot of that around here," she replied condescendingly.

Oh my God, she thinks I'm nutty, thought Paul.

"But … it really … happened."

The nurse laughed and said, "Well, give me a call next time you see them, okay? Now dinner is on its way. Can I get you anything?"

"Yes, a brain that works." Paul rolled his eyes, thinking, *I hope this speech thing settles down soon. They think I'm loony. I just can't get out the words I want to use.*

Paul spent the rest of the day reading the local newspapers and making a scrapbook of the stories that had been published over the past two weeks.

These stories were basically the same, describing the same alien creatures and providing descriptions of spaceships. There had been no stories, though, of children who had gone missing.

Paul had probably witnessed more that day than any other human had ever seen. That thought made him feel quite vulnerable. He wondered if the aliens knew that he had spied on them. He was about to find out.

By nine o'clock the next morning, physical therapy was finished for the day. Paul decided to wheel himself down to the lake near the forest. He took the book he was reading and his binoculars.

He'd only been sitting there for a few minutes, when a purple creature made its presence known. Paul was frightened and was about to call for help. The creature seemed to know this. It seemed to know what he was thinking and was able to talk with Paul telepathically. The creature asked Paul what the vehicle was that he was driving. Paul explained that it was a wheelchair and went on to explain the injuries he had sustained in the motor vehicle accident.

"So humans are unable to self-heal?" the creature asked.

Paul laughed. "No, we're not very good at healing the types of injuries I sustained. I mean, I have to relearn to talk properly, and I still don't know whether I will ever walk again."

Paul's Cure

The alien seemed to think deeply about this and cut off his communication with Paul. When he reconnected, he asked telepathically, "Would you like to be able to talk, hear, and walk again without difficulty?"

"Oh yes!" Paul thought hard to get his message across. "But it could take years and lots of surgery."

Reaching out his long arm and pointy finger, the alien rested it on Paul's head. He tapped gently a couple of times.

Paul said, "What do I do next?" Then he realised that he had just spoken the words and not merely thought them.

Next, the alien tapped his long finger on Paul's spine. To his absolute amazement, Paul was able to stand with no assistance at all.

"Wow, cool!" exclaimed Paul. "That was fantastic; I don't know how to thank you." He beamed.

"No need for thanks," replied the alien. "All you need to do is to tell your fellow humans that we are friendly and mean no harm to anyone."

"What about the children you took? Their parents are frantic and think they are gone forever!"

The purple alien look concerned. "I must apologise if people think we have stolen their children. We have only borrowed them for a few days. You see, our children were all killed by a virus, so we have no records of their achievements and milestones. In other words, we don't know what to expect. The few remaining children have been cloned, and we have used supports from the earth children to program our own children. This is so that they know how to be children—how to play, how to learn, how to love, and how to grow.

"We mean your children no harm at all, and they will be returned tomorrow with no knowledge of where they have been for the past few days."

"Brilliant," replied Paul. "Nobody saw the children being taken but me anyway, I don't think. If they're returned tomorrow, would it be okay for me to describe what happened to the local paper, so the people can be aware?"

The purple creature shook his head slowly. "I'm sorry, earthling, but I have to wipe your memory of our meeting. I can't allow you to share any of this with your fellow earthlings."

Paul was disappointed, but he was more than happy to accept his cured brain, his recovered hearing and comprehension, and his ability to walk. As soon as the alien had left him sitting there in his wheelchair, Paul had completely forgotten what they had discussed and the promises that the alien had made. Looking down, he realised that his body was moving. He lifted his left leg, then his right.

Wow! he thought. *I can move my legs.*

Very carefully he stood up, realising that he had completely recovered from his spinal injuries.

Nurse Callahan glanced out of the window and realised that Paul was standing unaided. She ran down the path towards the lake, shouting for Paul to sit back down, saying that he may fall over.

Paul smiled as she grew nearer. The nurse realised that she had never seen Paul smile like this before.

"I'm fine," said Paul. "My spinal injury seems to have resolved. I have no pain and no restricted movement as far as I can make out."

Nurse Callahan looked at Paul, stunned.

"Your speech!" she exclaimed. "It's completely recovered. Can you hear me properly?"

"Yes." Paul nodded. "I can hear you speak, and I understand what you're saying to me perfectly. I think I've mended completely."

Nurse Callahan, ever cautious, insisted on pushing Paul back to the ward, where doctors examined him from head to toe and were amazed to see that he was completely healed. It was some sort of miracle.

Paul had no recollection of the events of the day. However, when someone mentioned the missing children, he somehow knew that they would reappear very soon, totally unharmed. He couldn't work out how he knew this, so he kept quiet.

The hunt was on for ninety-seven missing children. There were very few clues as to their whereabouts. The area of land with the scorched fields was the subject of a very thorough line search by local police and members of the public. It failed to turn up any clues as to where the children might be.

Parents were beside themselves with grief, thinking that their children had been taken by some sort of cult followers, and most couldn't sleep for worry about what might be happening to their children at that very moment.

Daylight broke and a new search was commenced. Searching parties checked areas nearby and around the areas they had combed the day before.

The Children Return

The county fair was happening that weekend. Although nobody felt inclined to attend or do anything cheerful, police and some parents attended to see if any clues could be found of the missing children.

Barney Collins was spotted first by his father, who ran from one end of the fairgrounds to the other and hoisted his eight-year-old son onto his shoulders. "Barry's here. He's alive!" shouted his elated father.

The next moment, Mary Giles suddenly appeared on the merry-go-round. Police knew her from her photograph. The seven-year-old was promptly returned to her parents.

Peter Smith, Olive Boundy, Mark Stevens, Patrick O'Malley: they all reappeared seemingly from thin air. News quickly spread to other parents throughout the town, and before long all made haste for the fairgrounds, just in case.

By midafternoon all the children had reappeared and were being reunited with their families.

Not one child could give an explanation as to where they had been for the past two days. It was as if their memory of that period had been wiped completely. And regardless of health conditions before they'd disappeared, each child was now perfect. Any illness or birth defect they had before the abduction was cured completely.

Barry Collins's heart defect was gone; Olive Boundy's blindness was cured; Peter Smith no longer needed a kidney transplant …

It was indeed a succession of miracles. No one could work out how it had occurred.

The tall purple creature that had transported the children back telepathically smiled from his spaceship high up in the ionosphere and nodded to himself.

It was quid pro quo. For every piece of information gleaned from the borrowed earthlings, a cure for an illness was left in its place. Every tiny shred of DNA the aliens had taken from the earthling children meant the possibility of a regenerated population on their home planet ten million light years away.

The purple leader and his fellow travellers were looking forward to a future of bright, healthy, and happy purple children. The returned earth children could enjoy healthy and happy childhoods.

Quid pro quo. It seems that wherever we are in time and space, and whether we are human beings or tall purple space creatures, all we want in life for our children is a bright, happy, healthy future.

TAKE THE STAIRS!

The elevator door opened. I was looking downwards, as one does while waiting for what must be the slowest elevator in the world to arrive.

I wasn't the first person to scream. I looked up just as Mrs Brown pierced the air with her absolutely terrified squeal.

A crocodile—a bloody great crocodile. It rolled its eyes back lazily, as if disinterested, and flicked its tail from one side of the elevator to the other!

"*Bejaysus!*" I screamed (an exclamation left over from having an Irish father).

"*What the f ...*" I was bewildered, as bodies peeled off and headed for the safety of various offices. I fortunately had the presence of mind to press the elevator button to close the door, and then I hurried off not too far behind the others.

The crocodile carried on its journey upwards.

I dialled Pete, who was manning the reception desk that day. The phone was hastily snatched up at the same time as I heard Pete's ear-piercing scream. But the phone was off the hook. The crocodile had definitely exited the elevator this time. I wanted to drop the phone, because I could hear the sound of the crocodile crushing someone's bones, but I was glued to the spot.

"Pete! ... Pete! ... Pete, are you there? Are you okay?" I heard a thump, and the line went dead.

Jeez, what to do? What to do? Back on the phone, I felt was in some sort of nightmare and would wake up any second.

"What's your emergency? Fire, ambulance, or police?" chirped the friendly lady at the other end of the line.

"Yes. Police, ambulance, fire, army—I don't know. There's a great bloody crocodile in our office building, and I'm pretty sure it's killed at least one staff member, maybe more."

"Can you stay on the line safely?" she enquired.

"Yes."

"Good. Just make sure that the room you are in is locked, and stay there until the police arrive. Keep talking to me. Can you do that?" She was soothing my senses with her presence, albeit over the phone.

"Yes." I was shaking all over. I felt quite faint and immediately threw breakfast up and into the wastepaper bin. I kept hearing what I thought was Pete's skull being crushed.

"Okay, something's happening," I informed the woman on the telephone. I felt myself lift up a little at the sight of two policemen as they entered the floor. I put the phone back into its cradle and walked towards the door. The senior officer beckoned me as I cautiously opened the door a crack. I could have cried with joy at the sight of the officers' firearms on their utility belts. Even as I thought of my stand against guns, I knew that this was an exceptional case.

"What seems to be the problem?" the larger of the two enquired. He was six foot three and a mountain of pure muscle. His name tag told me that he was Sergeant Golden.

So I started to recount my bizarre tale, and he didn't bat an eyelid. "It happens," Sergeant Golden commented. "We get a bit of a drought and the pesky creatures venture into the storm water drains in search of water. Then sometimes they will venture further. They are as frightened of us as we are of them. Everybody screaming and shouting—it unnerves them."

The next twenty minutes or so was a flurry of excitement. The ambulance arrived only to pronounce poor old Pete officially eaten. Shortly after, a pair of Steve Irwin look-alikes arrived and had the croc trussed up and immobile in what seemed to be moments.

That was me finished for the day; I was emotionally and physically drained. I packed my briefcase and went to head off home. I walked to the elevator and then ... took the stairs instead!

I Spied a Yeti in the Bush today

I spied a Yeti in the bush today,

And there's no convincing me it wasn't real.

Out of every fake report, this has to be true.

When you truly examine the evidence,

The world is an insane place.

Every reporter is considered quite crazy, and

It doesn't seem to matter that

The evidence seems occasionally conclusive.

Some nutcase gives a false statement and ruins it for everyone.

And what makes it the truth?

Who says it's not all in the mind?

We think for now

That there will be real evidence one day.

Conditions will need to be optimal.

It's simply not fact that Yetis exist.

I don't doubt that you will agree that

We need to think realistically.

I doubt that even if you had eternal life,

You wouldn't say

"I spied a Yeti in the bush today."

(Now read it from bottom to top.)

THE FIFTH CHILD

It was noisy in the room, noisy and hot. And what on earth was that bright shining thing above them all?

Where she had just come from, it was dark and snug, and oh so quiet. Already the comforting *bump, bump, bump* of her mother's heartbeat was becoming a distant memory. She blinked, once, twice, three times—but everything was so hazy.

Then she turned her head, snuggled into her mother's arms, and felt immediately safe and secure. A slight nudge and an engorged button popped into her mouth, and suddenly there was an explosion of warm, silky magic, which she instinctively gulped greedily. *Hmm, maybe this isn't so bad after all!*

Oops, I spoke too soon! What? Wait! What? Wait! What on earth are they doing to my tummy? Oh my goodness, what are they? Snip, and the separation was complete.

Please, can I have the button back? Can I have the cuddly warm place back? Uh, uh … What's this stuff? I feel like I'm back inside Mummy's tummy, not all curled up but somehow floating in warm, wet liquid that smells kind of nice. I think the person with the funny hat said it was lavender … Oh, that must be my new favourite scent. I have a funny feeling that this is just the beginning of scents and sounds and sensations; of feeling warm and snug or wet and hungry; of slumber and wakefulness; of dozing and dreaming. This is the beginning of … life!

Julia Leigh was the fifth child born to Anne and Joseph Tanner of Liverpool, England. There were two older brothers, Jack and Paul, and two older sisters, Sophie and Mary.

Julia was born at full term (as were all of her other siblings) at Liverpool Maternity Hospital, after an unremarkable pregnancy. Her mum had simply turned up at the hospital on the nominated day, 16 July 1966, and four hours later Julia Leigh made her appearance.

At eight pounds and six ounces, she was her mother's largest baby, born with a shock of jet-black hair and the most beautiful pair of almond-shaped, piercing blue eyes. All Tanner children inherited their father's gorgeous blue eyes, varying in shape and size but as blue as cornflowers.

A quiet, placid babe, Julia Leigh achieved all of her milestones at the appropriate times and soon found her place within the bulging seams of the Tanner household. The older children adored her and fought for a cuddle whenever they could. Julia Leigh obliged by cooing and smiling and generally being very cute. Mummy made lots of cute little dresses for her, as she did for us older girls too, and there was always a cute bonnet to go with each outfit.

At four weeks, Julia Leigh was christened at St Marks Parish Church, just across the road from where we lived and where the siblings went to school. Her godparents were Brian Tanner (Dad's father) and his daughter Alice, and they travelled up from Essex for the occasion. Also there on the day were Aunty Sue and Uncle Martin and our cousins, Trudy and Annie. That being the case, there was a lovely big family gathering at home afterwards. Lots of noise, everyone trying to make themselves heard over the din of six children and a tired, overstimulated baby. Tiny triangular sandwiches, cheese, cold meats, pickled onions, crackers; the most gorgeous trifle—which was Mummy's specialty—and little cakes topped with lemon icing. Dandelion and burdock to wash it down, and a most welcome cup of tea for the women, while the menfolk "wet the baby's head" with an ale or two. A lovely day was had by all. A very tired little Julia Leigh was washed, changed, and fed and popped into her cot before the sun had gone down on the day.

MY AMAZING DREAM

The day broke on a glorious spring morning, with the beautiful Barossa Valley spread out below.

From my vantage spot I could see the gunmetal-grey sprinklers spring to life across the winery closest to me. The water created little rainbows across the vineyards.

I had been to this very spot many times in my dreams, but this was somehow more intense. I felt that I was going to learn something important here today.

Watching and waiting for something to happen, I spied the backpackers leaving the brightly coloured accommodation huts, walking two abreast and deep in conversation as they meandered down the track to the vineyard to commence picking for the day. The huts were fairly old, so the farmer gave the backpackers paint and allowed them to decorate the huts in any way they saw fit. This included street art or graffiti art, as long as there were no obscenities or "tagging". He was a good boss, old Costos, and paid his workers a fair wage for a good day's work.

I was rooted to the spot, as if I knew something wonderful was about to unfold.

The grapes were so full of juice that they looked as if they might burst any moment—and indeed they did. As I spied from my hiding place, I watched a young man reach for a bunch of red grapes. How he laughed as the grapes burst and exploded, leaving him with a strawberry wine "birthmark" on his already tanned face. The surprise on his face made me laugh along with him.

He looked around with wonder on his stained face. It was almost as though he could hear me laughing, but that wasn't possible, because this was a dream and I wasn't actually there. I was watching from outside the dream.

Strangely, an ochre dust storm started to gather in the east. How was that possible on such a beautiful, sunny day? There wasn't a cloud in the sky. Nor was there any wind. All was still, except for this dust storm, which was gathering momentum and growing in size as it drew nearer still.

The red dust flew upwards and outwards, as if to make a screen. The dust swirled and eddied and changed shape from a flat sheet to a three-dimensional figure. And there it was! I could see in the earthy dust a figure slowly taking form and shape. I gasped, tears streaming down my face, grief shuddering through my very core.

It was an epiphany. Dressed in her favourite forest green jumper and jeans, it was my beautiful sister Karen. She was shouting to me. I panicked. I couldn't hear her, so I tried to stand up. The image started to fade. Karen held up her hand as if to tell me to sit back down, so I obliged, mesmerised.

Once again the image became clear. Karen was smiling her cheeky, beautiful smile and she started to talk to me. I could hear her clearly now.

"I was too young to leave you all." She smiled sadly. "I know you all miss me terribly, even though I've been gone for nine years today, but I'm happy enough. I have my mum and Harry to keep me company. I've watched my grandchildren being born and growing up. I wish I'd met them, and I have in a way. They know me from photos and stories, and I watch over them every day. Tell Amy I'm so proud of her. She's an amazing mother, wife, and daughter, and she grows more beautiful every day."

I started to cry again.

"My darling sister, don't cry. We will be together again one day. In the blink of an eye we are gone, and when our time on earth is done, we can start a new life up here."

She lifted both of her hands, palms upwards, to signify surroundings that I couldn't see.

"Tell Ben that I love him and miss him and that he has turned into the man I wanted him to become. I'm proud of his achievements, and he is so talented in his work.

"Tell Carl that I'm happy that he found love a second time. I'm so glad that he's not alone and that he has a wonderful, kind, and loving wife to keep him warm on cold nights. He was too young to be alone forever."

"Fiona?"

"Yes?" I lifted my head up to take in the image of her fully. She was as beautiful as when she was a girl of sixteen.

"Don't cry for me. Be happy. And I'm saving a spot next to me for you, so that one day we can be as thick as thieves once again." She laughed that tinkling, beautiful sound I'd missed so much but could never forget.

Suddenly I remembered that I was dreaming and I was sitting on this craggy grey rock waiting for a message. "What did you want to tell me?" I enquired. The image was starting to fade.

"Don't go, Karen. Please stay." I remembered begging with these same words nine years ago.

"It's okay," Karen replied, fading faster. "I just wanted you to know that when Carl scattered my ashes over the valley from the hot air balloon, this is where my heart landed. You are sitting exactly in that place, where the dust from my stilled heart settled." Her silhouette was all that remained now. I knew that any second she would be gone.

"Goodbye again, my darling sister," she whispered softly, fading now, until there was just a tiny cloud right above my head.

"Goodbye, Karen, 'til we meet again one day. I love you and miss you always."

"I love you too," she whispered quietly, and then faded away completely.

I was bereft. The tears came as though they would never stop. Then I looked out over the valley and knew that she was here and always would be. At rest, she was pain-free and watching over us all. A rainbow stretched from one side of the valley to the other. *How bizarre,* I thought; *it hasn't even rained today.* Then I remembered that Karen loved rainbows and she had sent this message to me, to us …

"If you see a rainbow, I will be holding one end in my hand, and you will know that I am watching over you and that you are safe."

I stole one last look over the valley. I took in all the shades of green and the patchwork shapes of the vineyards and farms—a myriad of shades and hues in every direction. Looking down, I realised that the rock I was sitting on was now earthy red. I also realised that this was the spot that held Karen's heart. I smiled, and a deep sense of relaxation and comfort washed over me.

As I rolled over and opened my eyes, I thought, *Wow what a powerful dream!* It was a dream, wasn't it?

AUTOPSY REVEALS

Lisa lay in the middle of the floor in a pool of mixed bodily fluids. The autopsy revealed that she was lying her own blood and vomit, and his urine.

Her partner Sean had apparently arrived home the night before after a long session at the local pub and his behaviour was seemingly out of character.

Neighbours heard the whole thing and rang the police.

Julia, who was interviewed by police, said that she heard Sean shouting. He'd said, "Who've you been sleeping with, you whore?"

Lisa had replied, "What? No one but you, Sean. I'm not interested in anyone else."

"Lying, stinking whore," he'd yelled. Lisa had heard the crunch as he knocked out her front tooth.

"They're all talking about you at the pub. They say you've been sleeping with your personal trainer!" Sean screamed.

Lisa pleaded to be heard. "Of course I'm not, Sean," she said, through blood and missing teeth. "I'll change to another trainer if you want me to. I don't know why people are saying those things."

"Fuck you, you bitch. I don't believe anything you say!" Sean screamed. Lisa heard another crash. The autopsy suggested he had pulled her head up by the hair and smashed it into the concrete.

It was then that she must have lost consciousness and mercifully missed the fact that he was urinating over her inert body: the ultimate degrading act.

Cause of death: massive brain trauma sustained by having her head slammed continually into a concrete floor.

KARMA

Beep, beep, beep, beep.

What? What's that? Dave thought to himself.

Oh God, it's the alarm … five o'clock and I have a breakfast meeting at Minna Mia at seven.

Dave rolled over, trying to shake the fog from his brain, scratching his balls in the process.

What the …? My balls have disappeared! How is that possible?!

He snaked his hand slowly upwards and realised, *Oh, Christ, my dick has gone too!*

Dave was wide awake now.

Wait … What's this? I have a vagina!

Jumping out of bed, Dave cracked his shin on the dresser, and yelping, realised that he no longer had hairs on his legs, or anywhere else, except on his scalp, where he had grown a mass of long, silky, golden tresses! And there was a little triangle of hair between his thighs. It was almost as if the rest of his body had been waxed.

Daring himself to look into the mirror on the wall, Dave discovered that he had not only a nice neat little pubic package but also huge boobs, and a tiny waist to go with them.

Jesus!

Dave tore his eyes away from his newly acquired female parts. He was suddenly face-to-face with a familiar, yet unknown, person staring back at him.

I'm confused. It looks like me, but it isn't. How can this be? It's me with female body parts … No, it's me, and I've turned into a woman. Not too bad-looking either, he thought to himself.

Stop it! This is impossible! How can I go to bed as a man, with all of the anatomical bits and pieces that go with it, and wake up a shapely gorgeous woman? He winked at himself in the mirror, then looked at himself in horror.

Stop it, you idiot; you're winking at yourself!

Oh God, Julie was right, I'm a male chauvinistic pig and treat women like my own private property—and this is my punishment!

Last evening, at his best mate Jack's birthday party, Dave and Julie had consumed a couple of bottles of Cabernet Sauvignon and were both pretty drunk. Dave was sleazing all over Julie's friend Tully, and Julie was furious.

"You'll never change, Dave. I don't know why I put up with it," Julie had yelled at him while they were standing outside waiting for the taxi.

"What?" Dave enquired innocently. "You know you're the only one I love. What does a bit of harmless flirting do?" Dave winked at her and gave her what he thought was his sexiest smile.

Julie gave a frustrated groan. "You don't get it, do you? Every time you sleaze over one of my mates, you leave me looking foolish for being involved with you. You embarrass me with your behaviour."

"But it's only harmless fun!" Dave laughed, and winked at Julie again, attempting to fold her up in his arms and smooth things over, slobbering over her with boozy kisses.

"No, leave me alone. I think it's about time we thought about where this relationship is going. If you were serious about me, you wouldn't feel the need to sleaze all over my friends.

"You need a taste of your own medicine, but I'm not inclined that way. I could no more cheat on you than fly! Maybe a break would do us good. We can have some space and work out where this relationship is going!"

With that, Julie jumped into the next cab and left Dave weaving unsteadily on the footpath, contemplating his future. More importantly, he wondered how he was going to get home.

The scene was playing over and over in Dave's brain as he turned back to the bedroom to talk, to find that Julie had not come back to his apartment. He could only assume that she had gone home. They did spend the occasional night apart, but it seemed to be less and less these days.

Dave realised that he had possibly done irreparable damage to his relationship. This worried him. He truly loved Julie and didn't want to lose her. He didn't know how to handle the situation, and he couldn't face work today, so he rang his mate Terry and asked him to fill in for him at the breakfast meeting. Terry, only too happy to oblige, signed off so he could get showered and dressed and go over the notes that Dave had emailed to him.

Next, Dave called into work, saying that he had some pressing family issues and needed a couple of days off. He was happy to use up his annual leave days. That posed no problems to him either.

Dave knew that he needed to apologise to Julie and let her know that he didn't want to lose her. He would do anything to prevent her from leaving the relationship.

At the moment, though, he needed a good hot shower. And then he needed to call his best buddy Jack to talk about his metamorphosis. Jack could be trusted to be discreet. And at least he wouldn't laugh at Dave's predicament. Jack was a psychiatrist, and Dave assumed that he'd seen it all. If memory served Dave correctly, Jack had taken a few days off to do some jobs around the house. Dave picked up his phone and dialled Jack's number.

"Hi, this is Jack speaking. I'm unable to get to the phone right now, but I'll get back to you as soon as possible …"

Darn, thought Dave, *he's probably gone for his early morning run. I'll give him an hour and try again.*

After leaving a message on Jack's phone, Dave padded into the kitchen and was just reaching up for the cereal in the pantry when a fierce cramping sensation doubled him over the kitchen bench.

Oh my God, I'm dying! He groaned inwardly.

Then as soon as it had appeared, it disappeared again, and he thought no more about it.

Sitting at the breakfast bar, Dave struggled to get down a bowl of cereal. Usually he would be ravenously hungry after a night on the tiles, but now he felt strangely disinterested in food.

Argh, there it goes again. Maybe I have appendicitis … He rushed off to the bathroom thinking he was going to throw up.

Making it to the bathroom without a technicolour yawn made him feel a bit better. He stepped over to the toilet to urinate. Forgetting what had happened that morning, he reached down to aim and was reminded all over again that it was still missing. This time, he did throw up—and there were the cramps again!

Dave turned around, realising that he now had to sit to use the toilet, and remembering that he now also had to use toilet paper to dry his nether regions. Almost passing out from the sight of the blood on the toilet paper, he inhaled with fright.

Fuck me dead, I cannot believe what is happening to me! Not only do I have a snatch and boobs, but now I'm having a period into the bargain! How is that even anatomically possible? And what do I do about it?

Dave found some tampons in the bathroom that Julie had left behind. He tried to insert the tampon, realising finally that the wrapper had to be removed first.

Oh my God, that hurts. How do women put these things inside them for one week out of four, from adolescence to menopause? At least I know I'm not pregnant! He chuckled, then admonished himself for doing so. Just then the phone rang. Dave snatched it up.

"Hi, Dave speaking."

"Hi, Dave, it's me returning your call," replied Jack. "Are you okay? You sound a bit weird."

"Jack, can you please come over to my apartment? … Please … Like, right now?"

Jack turned serious. "What's going on, buddy? Are you in some kind of trouble? You didn't take a girl home with you, did you? Julie will have your balls on a plate!"

Dave gave short, dry snort. "I don't think so, buddy. Just come over now … please!"

Jack had never heard Dave sound like this. He knew it was serious, whatever was bugging his friend, so he agreed to come right over.

"I'll see you in twenty minutes, okay, Dave?" He thought that Dave was going to burst into tears, so he quickly put the phone down and grabbed some clothes, dashing out to his car five minutes later.

Dave contemplated phoning Julie but realised that she'd still be angry with him. Besides which, he had no idea how to explain the changes to his body just yet, so he thought he'd better wait, at least until he'd spoken to Jack.

True to his promise, Jack pulled up in the driveway. Dave attempted to compose himself as he walked slowly to the front door to let him in.

"Hi, buddy …" Jack stopped in midsentence.

I must look a sight, thought Dave. *Not only am I in my own daggy boxers and T-shirt, with my giant boobs poking through the front, but also my hair—my hair hasn't been brushed and probably resembles a haystack after having been vacated by a group of teenagers. I must look a complete mess. To make matters worse, I'm about to burst into tears.* He looked downward to ward off the waterworks.

Jack stood in the doorway, not exactly entering, but not backing away either. For what was probably the first time in his life, he was speechless. Then his professionalism took over.

"Hi, buddy. I got here as soon as I could. You sounded a bit stressed … Everything okay?"

Dave looked at his friend, who had known him since nursery school. His mouth opened and closed, but no words came out. He reminded himself of a goldfish.

"It's okay, Dave, I understand. Lots of men go through the same thing. A bit of cross-dressing, artificial boobs, and a nice wig can go a long way to satisfy their curiosity …"

"No!" Dave held up his hand to silence his friend. "I don't know what happened to me, but I woke up like this. They are not fake boobs, and this is not a wig. And Jesus, Jack, what am I going to do?" Dave collapsed into a flood of tears as Jack followed him into the house.

It was Jack's turn to look like a goldfish, his mouth opening and closing. He had never encountered a situation like this before in all of his professional or personal life.

"What happened last night, Dave?" asked Jack. "Because whatever it was seems to have triggered these changes, hormonal, physiological, or spiritual. Whatever it is, something powerful has taken place."

Dave told his friend the story of the night before. He felt deeply ashamed of his actions, not just for last night but also for all of the embarrassment he had caused to Julie. He only hoped that it was not too late to salvage the relationship.

Dave and Jack spent the entire day talking. Dave knew that he needed to grow up and show respect for the woman he loved. Julie, he realised, was the woman he wanted to marry and spend the rest of his life with. Could he salvage the relationship?

He was fairly clear that he couldn't go to visit her in this current state, so he sent a dozen red roses with an inscription of love penned onto the card. In his mind he also wanted to apologise for his behaviour, not just for last night but also for all of the other times that he had embarrassed and humiliated her.

"Jack, do you mind if we go for a walk and get a bit of fresh air?" It was almost dinner time, so Dave changed into a pair of his jeans and a really loose sweatshirt. He tied his hair back in a ponytail. Then they wandered down to Dave's local watering hole.

Halfway down the block, a couple of builders knocking off for the day gave a long, low wolf whistle. Dave coloured bright red, aware that it was intended for him.

"Why do men have to humiliate women in this manner? It's so disrespectful," Dave said to Jack, who raised his eyebrows and said nothing.

As they reached the pub, the Golden Admiral, they were greeted by ushers who thought that the pair had turned up for trivia night. The place was packed.

As they fought their way through the crowd, Dave felt his bottom being given a squeeze or a gentle pat. He was furious that men showed no respect for women. If he'd actually seen the culprits, he would have told them so himself.

They found a table, and Jack went up to the bar and ordered both of their meals. As if this were a signal that Dave was available, a very drunk man made a beeline for him. Pushing his face up against Dave's, the man slobbered beery kisses on his cheeks.

Okay, yuk, this is exactly what Julie was complaining about. How could I embarrass her in this way? A fresh set of tears was hovering on Dave's eyelids, threatening to roll down his cheeks at any second.

Jack arrived back at their table. Fairly quickly they had their meals set in front of them. They ate in the comfortable silence that only two people who've known each other all their lives can sustain.

After they had eaten their fill and slaked their thirst with a couple of beers, Dave explained to Jack how the events of the day had shaped up.

"I am totally ashamed of myself, Jack. I have no idea why Julie is still with me, if in fact she still is. I can't see her entering into a lesbian relationship, so if I'm stuck in this body, then it appears that I've lost the love of my life. If only I'd realised that before I allowed things to deteriorate to this level. Julie's right, I'm a male chauvinist pig and I don't deserve a wonderful woman like her."

Dave had had a few beers now and there was an increased risk that he would burst into a fresh bout of tears, so Jack made the suggestion that they start to head home.

Upon arriving home, Dave wondered whether he should call Julie and apologise once again. Jack, however, talked him around and suggested a good night's sleep before facing Julie. There had been no response from his text message, so she may still be angry with him.

Jack stayed with Dave. They downed a couple of shots of port, Dave growing sleepier by the minute. Pretty soon he fell into a deep sleep on the sofa.

Good, thought Jack.

Sorry, buddy. I know I'm your best mate, but I've done this out of love and respect for both you and Julie. I could see the way you were carrying on last night, and I knew it was just a matter of time before Julie had enough and gave you the flick for good.

Jack sat down quietly beside Dave and reversed the hypnotic spell he'd performed on him the previous night—the hypnosis that convinced him that he'd turned into a woman, with all of the anatomical parts that went with the fairer sex, the spell that convinced him that he was suffering from menstrual cramps and the need to use tampons. He had been convinced that men had disrespectfully wolf whistled at him and it had humiliated him. He also felt certain that men had groped him in the pub and made boozy, disgusting advances towards him, and he'd felt embarrassed for all the times he'd done the same things himself.

Would the changes that Jack had instilled in Dave's thought processes be permanent? Well, it would become evident in time.

Jack stood up and grabbed a blanket, draping it over his best mate. As he did so, he was fascinated that although no changes had occurred to Dave's body, he was absolutely convinced that they had.

Okay, let's hear it for the powers of persuasion!

"Sleep tight, my friend. You'll remember nothing of all this tomorrow, but your thoughts will be changed forever. There will be no more flirting or any behaviour that humiliates Julie. No more getting plastered and drooling over other women. Dave, you will be the best boyfriend that Julie has ever had. You don't want to let this one slip through your fingers. Ask her to marry you. Why shouldn't you be as miserable as the rest of us?" He chuckled. "Goodnight, Dave."

Jack let himself out and left Dave snoring on the sofa, where he spent the entire night.

Beep, beep, beep, beep.

What? … What's that? Dave thought to himself.

Oh God, it's the alarm … five o'clock and I have a breakfast meeting at Minna Mia at seven o'clock. Why am I sleeping on the sofa?

Dave rolled over, trying to shake the fog from his brain, scratching his balls in the process and giving a gentle tug on his morning erection.

Oh jeez, I was an ass last night. I'd better give Julie a call and apologise profusely. It's about time I grew up a bit, I think. If I want Julie to be my bride … What? Where did that idea come from?

I do though. I do want Julie to marry me, and when I get married it's going to be for keeps! There will be no more flirting, or anything that will cause embarrassment to Julie. I'm giving myself to her completely, and I'll show her that I love, honour, and respect her—forever!

That was an odd dream I had last night, but it's put things into perspective, and I intend to rectify all past mistakes.

Why do I feel that Jack has something to do with my dream?

Printed in the United States
By Bookmasters